Hand of Mercy

Ni Claydon

Copyright

©2008 Ni Claydon

ISBN 978-1-4092-3288-9

Dedication

To my beautiful and devastatingly intelligent niece Abigail, who is certainly too young to read this yet!

Acknowledgements

The cover and the author photo were both taken by G.D. Smart, one drizzly day in Nottingham. Further artwork can be found here:
http://www.tigermoth-art.co.uk/

Proofreading and general comma wrangling was done by Natalie Hayes in a variety of British cities.

In the depths of Wales lives the Sturrock family, who kindly allowed me to get a large amount of writing done in their home while discussing plot ideas with Nuala the dog.

Prologue

1490

Splendid in his glory, infinite in his mercy, the blade that killed without wounding, Clemael walked forth upon the earth.
Well, on the thick bed of rushes and straw that stretched the length of the hallway. Clemael was barely able to touch the base clay, even in his heavy sandals.
He looked around curiously. Stable, almost certainly. From the next stall over, a horse of some quality whickered a welcome to the visitor, before returning to its fresh-smelling hay.
Clemael stepped cautiously from the stable. The cobbled pavement outside indicated that this wasn't a public stable, but a series of buildings connected to the early-Tudor glory of the manor house rising on a low incline in front of him.
Remembering the last time he walked in England, Clemael kept an eye out for any rose-badges, and wasn't surprised to see that over the lintel of the gate was a five-petalled rose that had recently had five new outer petals inexpertly carved. York and Lancaster no longer mattered, and Clemael found himself pleased by this.
Still, a mystery remained. Who were the voices in the dark, screaming his name over and over as a whip came down?
Unlike a lot of his brothers in the Host, Clemael didn't simply rush in. He took the time to circle the manor house warily, noting the good state of repair, and the utter silence inside. The horse indicated money, the house even more so, so why were there no servants, no masters, not a single human indication to be found?
The silence was starting to settle along Clemael's shoulder,

keeping them oppressed and heavy. If he chose to unfold his wings now, he would have found them difficult to rai-
Mad laughter filled the lawn.
Clemael jumped- and then realised it was nothing worse than birds calling out from one tree to another. Angry with himself, he shook himself and considered the best way to enter the house.
I startled like an ephemeral, he thought crossly. If I get out of this in one piece, I'm going to spend a day dreaming of singing the Te Deum with everyone else fresh out of the cauldron.
There was a window open. Even better, it was a window filled in with strips of translucent horn rather than glass, which suggested it was more likely to be a servant's quarters than anywhere particularly well guarded. Well, all right, with guards used to guarding anything more difficult than a stick of cinnamon.
Easing the horn out of the window, Clemael put a hand on the wall beneath, and considered hauling himself in-
The wall burned.
Staring into the room, half-paralysed by something he didn't understand, Clemael saw there were lines on the walls, markings, scraps of three different alphabets. Words of restraint, imprisonment, and pain. Without looking, Clemael knew that his hand had landed on one of the charcoal incantations, trapping him like a fox in a bear trap.
Clemael was breathing, no, panting. He felt that probably wasn't helping matters, and stilled his lungs until they stopped distracting him. That was how he heard the click of an inner door, and then a closer one, before the door into the room he'd half entered slid against a stone.
The newcomer looked Clemael up and down. "The Angel of Mercy, I do believe. Well worth getting my acolytes to torture

themselves in your name." The newcomer stepped into the light, and Clemael could see the restless eyes above the greying beard. "That's nothing compared to what they're going to do to you, though, not now their blood lust has awoken. Is it true angels are not possessed of the things of men? You will disappoint them, though it's possible they'll carve their own passageways within you, regardless. One has already vouchsafed that he'll pour the sweepings of the streets over you, and drown you in pigs' blood."

Clemael made no reply. The newcomer shrugged. "No words yet, I suppose it's as well you've not started the pleading yet. Plenty of time for that. For you, you have failed in your charge, Angel of Mercy. You left us, all humanity, in this filth, in this anguish." There were tears in his eyes. "How is that merciful? So you will wear the iron chains of slavery, you'll be betrayed for too little silver, choked on mercury, denied your gold. And when we have aged and died, and our sons have aged and died, and our grandsons have tired of this broken toy that used to be all light and beauty, only then will you understand what it's like to live as a man in the light of your supposed mercy."

Lungs filled once again. Clemael was a Potence, after all, not one of those chubby-baby angels but the older kind that laid waste to whole cities and sang glorious symphonies of praise as the topless towers burned and crumbled.

With his free hand, Clemael reached up toward heaven, and prayed for a blade.

It appeared instantly, a slim pillar of orange flame balanced precariously on a metal hilt. Without giving himself time to think, Clemael ignored the scream of rage from indoors, and swept the blade downwards, over his own wrist.

There was a sound both wet and meated, and Clemael's trapped hand landed inside the room. The flesh melted away like beeswax as it fell, so that in less than a minute there was a series of tiny clicks as the exposed bones settled onto the floor.

With a whumph of wings unfurling, Clemael kicked away from the ground, away from the house and the trap he'd nearly succumbed to. The wound was already cauterised by the flame, so he counted himself lucky. And hey, he didn't even have to sing the sing the Te Deum, he most certainly was not in one piece.

Free of vanity, it didn't yet occur to Clemael to miss his hand.

One is for the lead, lifted holy high,
Two is for copper, the bath of maids who die.

Three is for the tin, and knockings in the dark,
Four is for mercury, ageing in the park.

Five is for iron, the knight that learnt to sing.
Six is for silver, the temple of the king.

Seven is the gold, the hallow of the spear,
These the bones of mercy for the hand that we must fear.

Chapter One

I take the opening and closing times of the shop from the grandfather clock next to the till. All right, I check it against the radio sometimes, but generally it does a good job noting the hours while people shop at the farmers' market every Thursday, or else generally potter round the genteel town centre.
It's for sale, of course, but the little tag swinging from the keyhole is bleached from the sun, the ink fading away. Like a few of the stock items in my tiny antique shop, I'd be sorry to see it gone. There's some French silverware that catches the light when I open the blinds of a morning, that dazzle wakes me up better than a double espresso.
I flipped the sign, and did a little half-hearted vacuum cleaning of the carpet, watching the dust whirl round the innards of the machine in an end-of-day reverie. It's hard to describe the colour of the carpet, the best most people could do is "probably started off brown." I'd replace it given half the chance, but this isn't my shop yet, and I really hope it won't be for a while yet. The sign over the door says Asherwood Antiques, and old Mr Asherwood himself is in Bluebell Park Retirement Village, growing ever more confused at the world. I made a mental note to visit him on Sunday. I wasn't always great about remembering, all those bright flowers they encouraged the residents to grow and tend couldn't disguise the general hopelessness of the place. But I was clearly more diligent than his only child, because last time she bothered showing up the nurses reckoned she was an impostor, since the "frizzy-haired girl with the stick" was clearly his daughter. I wasn't thrilled by

"frizzy-haired", in fact I made sure I wore my hair in a plait for all future visits.

That particular day, I had the till counted out, and was out of the shop by ten past five, which I considered a small miracle. It meant I could gratefully scramble onto the bus as soon as it arrived with a squeal of brakes and a hiss of the suspension lowering. I like to see a lowering step; if my kneecaps powder away much more I'm going to be in a wheelchair before I'm very much older.

A couple of people shifted out of my way, a polite reflex in the face of the stick. I kept my shopping from lunchtime on my lap, and watched the hedgerows go by until the stop closest to Nana Sophie's new house.

For the rest of my life, I'm going to expect Nana Sophie to be living in a bungalow in the middle of nowhere, keeping a couple of half-feral hens and a country-style kitchen bigger than my my entire flat. About seven years ago, though, she sold off her house and land with a big sigh of relief, and moved to a new housing estate with public transport links, nearby shops, and most blessedly of all, central heating. It's a nice house she has now, but it's not very...granny.

But then, neither is she.

I let myself into the house. Nana Sophie doesn't lock herself away; my Dad fitted a burglar chain to the front door when she moved in, but to my knowledge she's never bothered with it. I picked my way past what was probably half a ton of computer components, and grinned at the electrical hum rising from the front room. She'd been upgrading again, then. Nana Sophie was always keen on information technology, she'd eventually developed a skill at applying a soldering iron and gaffer tape in a manner that voided every warranty ever written.

There was a mumble of voices in the kitchen, so I headed there, already fetching a chocolate cake out of the shopping I'd brought. Visiting Sophie added at least a stone to my weight, I was convinced.

I opened the door.

I couldn't work out what I was seeing.

Nana Sophie was as straight as a blade. The congenital bone defect that killed her daughter and crippled her grand-daughter was clearly not present in her, and for the first time I saw that Nana Sophie must have been a beauty in her prime, in the old way of Greek nymphs and Arcadian maidens. She was staring into the all-pervading light as though it was just a candle.

The light, it didn't have a source, but it fell on my skin like sunlight must have when the stars were young and excited about all their possibilities. The shine of it was backlighting a male form; it was hard to make out the details of face and age. But there was a line of the light underneath the soles of his shoes, which meant he had to be floating just above the floor, perhaps no more than an inch or so.

I didn't think, I just threw the chocolate cake at him. The pure sense of something being strange and wrong near my Nana made me throw myself across the gap after the cake, waving my stick. I'm not sure what I shouted, something incoherent about leaving her alone. As far as I'm concerned, what I shouted was clearly too magnificent and witty for any one's memory's to hold.

The man caught my shoulders.

"Are you all right miss?" he asked, passing me my miraculously unharmed chocolate cake. "Did you stumble? Let me get you a chair."

I gaped at him. Close up, I had expanses of pale, smooth skin and the smell of new pillows.

Nana Sophie took the cake, and slid it onto the big round plate traditionally holding court on the kitchen table. "I told you, Clem, showing off won't get you anywhere. Now sit down like a civilised creature and have some cake."

Clem and I look at each other, abashed. Wordlessly, he released my shoulders, and held out a chair for me. "After you, miss."

The last thirty seconds had me so thoroughly bewildered, I sat down without even wondering if he was going to snatch away the chair at the last moment.

In his light grey suit and stylish driving gloves, Clem's age was hard enough to determine, but when he'd been told off by Sophie he'd looked my age. Now, taking a seat, he looked closer to hers. Not so much in terms of sudden, obvious wrinkles, but more grey, more used-up in a way the young seldom manage unless they've had a very bad life.

"Glass of milk for you, Helen," Nana Sophie passed the glass and a four-pint bottle of semi-skimmed over to me. Normally, I didn't mind Nana Sophie talking to me like a school kid, but in front of Clem I shuffled like the fifteen-year-old I'd been ten years ago. A decade, already!Some part of me kept mentally checking my age, because in my head I'm sometimes thirteen and shy around boys, or else fifty and considering a walking frame.

"I imagine the calcium helps," said Clem neutrally. Nana Sophie shot him a warning glance.

"Don't you mind Clem," said Nana Sophie,slicing through the cake with a triangular blade. "He just wants me to give him a hand." Her mouth twisted slightly, in a faint, private amusement.

Clem stood up. "Thank you, Chok, it seems clear to me I've come to the wrong place. I won't trouble you further."

"Oh, sit down." Sophie put three small plates out, and awkwardly levered out the first slice of cake. "You know damn

well I don't get involved in the old firm's little squabbles. Besides, if you want to find scented things, you use a hound, and if you want to use holy things, you use a human."
Clem nearly snorted. "Ah yes, I shall pick one of the multitude of humans in my social circle, and persuade them of many, many impossible things."
"Why are you talking like you're not human?" I nearly didn't notice Nana Sophie holding out a cake-laden plate to me. "Oh wait, that would be the glowing and floating. I didn't imagine that, did I?" I started edging myself between Clem and Nana Sophie, but she chuckled and put the plate down in front of me.
"There," she said with satisfaction. "That's why Helen's weekly visits are never dull. And often calorific. Go on, Clem, persuade her of impossible things."
"That's okay," I started, scared of something happening I couldn't cope with. "I'm ready to belie-"
There were three small pops, and looking down I saw Clem unfastening his driving gloves. Heavy old-fashioned articles, then he slapped on the table before showing me his hands. The left hand was pale, fine-fingered with skin smooth as milk, no palm or finger prints, no line for gimcrack tellers to declaim over. Nonetheless, there was a tiny suggestion of wrinkles around the knuckles, presumably just from where he'd been moving the fingers.
The other hand...at first I thought it was an ice sculpture, but he unconsciously flexed the fingers, and the light shifted inside. The fact that he could flex the fingers and wrist without any hinges or angles were strange enough, because his left hand was one solid piece of quartz. There were tiny layers and inclusions in it- feathers and clouds, as my jeweller friends would call them. It made the mineral look organic, or at least less bewildering than the sight of solid stone moving with the

agility of muscle and bone would have been.
Even half-hypnotised by the play of light inside the false hand, I found a voice. "What are you?"
Nana Sophie finished her cake slice. "He is Clemael. And he was created to be the Angel of Mercy."
"Both my created purpose, and my pleasure." The words were slightly smug, but Clem's earnest tone made them seem boyishly enthusiastic.
"Woah," I said faintly.
"If that's really the best you can do in terms of awe and wonder," even sitting down, Clem sketched me a little half bow, "then I am appropriately flattered."
Recovering, I gave him a sardonic look. "Hard to be awed of someone who's got chocolate cake all round his chops." He didn't, but his slight fluster as he produced a handkerchief made me feel better. Nana Sophie cackled in a corner.
I took of sip of milk, and a small and largely irrelevant part of my brain was glad it wasn't that soy stuff Nana Sophie took a liking to last year. There's such a thing as too much virtue in a room. "So, do all angels have a crystal hand?"
"No," Clem sighed in the general direction of his gloves. "I...lost it. To a human magician. It's a bit traumatic." He shuddered, and again looked the same age as my grandmother. "But the bones remain somewhere, and need recovering."
Nana Sophie stood up in one fluid movement, and pulled a note off the door of the fridge. "Sir Elgar's notes only make one mention of your hand, Clem. It's in the form of a riddle, and in Latin besides, but translating the worst of it wasn't too bad. It seems that his initial plan was to use the entire hand, he called it the Hand of Mercy. In the end, his greed got the better of him, ended up selling a joint here, a finger here."
I squinted at what looked like bad poetry. "So this is how he

remembered who the, what, the buyers were?"
"More like what they did with the bits." Nana Sophie pressed the paper into my palm. It's the same way she used to press five pound notes into my hand for my birthdays.
Come to think of it, she still did.
"And they're all still in this country?" Clem was nearly fidgeting with impatience.
"On this island," Sophie corrected him gently.
I read one line three times, felt a grin break out over my face. "This Mercury one... hey, do we have to find these bits in order?" I stopped an saw Clem's expression. "Yeah, all right, I used 'we'. Stop smirking and answer the question."
Clem took the paper from me, and smiled. "I don't see why we should have to. Shall we go tomorrow?"

Chapter Two

Sundays are my days. The antiques shop was closed, the town centre not having much truck with the more lenient Sunday trading laws. Traditionally, this was a day involving nothing more strenuous than cooking a lamb shank and maybe some red wine and mint gravy.
So the knock at the door at ten was not best welcome.
Despite my general disarray, I made a point of walking steadily to the door. My knees have had the benefit of not taking weight for eight hours, or at any rate four or five hours when the painkillers couldn't cut it. Either way, later on in the day I'd be nearly in tears of gratitude for knees that felt as well as they did right now, so I appreciated them as much as I could.
Clem was waiting in perfect, composed patience. Again, his outfit was light grey, but there was a precisely creased quality that suggested he probably owned- or maybe incarnated?- a selection of slightly different suits.
"Oh bugger," I told him feelingly. "I thought I'd dreamt you."
He eyed my hair, and my dressing gown. I'll bet angels don't own, incarnate or have anything to do with pink fluffy dressing gowns with smiling flowers embroidered on one side. And while I'm prepared to concede that pink lost it's magnetic attraction when I turned twelve, when I've spent all week in sensible, slightly restrictive shop-manager clothes, I like pink and fluffy on my day off.
"Good morning," Clem kept his voice pitched low. "We agreed to meet today; you knew the location of one or more of the bones."
"Huh. Yeah. Let me get a shower and some clothes. Got a car?"
Clem spread his hands. "I have other means of transportation,

but for this we might need Shank's pony."
I checked my walking stick was in it's usual place behind the door. "Shank's pony got sent to the glue factory some years back. We're getting a bus."

As it stood, there were worse places to end up than Bluebell Park Retirement Village.
Village was a bit of misnomer, though. It was four houses arranged around a courtyard, the main house being the original building. In the main house was the reception, hospital, and various offices. The big old conservatory along the back length served as a communal dining hall for those who fancied a bit of company.
The only problem, so far as I was concerned, was that the 'village' was right next door to the parish church, complete with the inevitable graveyard. I'm sure they didn't mean to go with the obvious resemblance to a production line. On Sundays you can see a crocodile of old dears being led to and from services, like a small, grumbling school trip.
Mr. Asherwood lived in one of the smaller buildings, Ivy Cottage. Their impersonal architecture always reminded me of student halls, except that my halls had more stairs, and definitely more interesting posters.
He was in the living room, being cajoled by a nurse. "Now, Mr Asherwood, some residents enjoy their soaps."
"Rots the brain!" Mr. Asherwood was going quite purple in the face. "There's a documentary on Civil War firearms, and I-"
"That's got a lot of loud bangs, some of the other residents might be frightened. Do try to think of other people, Mr. Asherwood." The nurse was nearly cooing.
I found I was grinning. "It's one of his good days," I whispered to Clem. "Some days you can sort of see the man he used to be,

before he took ill."

The nurse saw me, and couldn't keep the relief off her face. "Look, Mr. Asherwood, you have visitors. See, here's your friend Helen."

Mr. Asherwood tottered across to me, and took my hands like a favourite uncle. "Helen, my dear girl. This simpering harridan wants me to dissolve my brains on the make-believe lives of vacuous teenagers. Hmph." He pulled at the sleeves of his jackets. "Come along, Miss Hawthorn, let's go speak somewhere more congenial."

Clem took my arm as I allowed Mr. Asherwood to lead me off. He still had deep reservations about inviting a young lady into what amounted to his bedroom, but it was either that or the communal areas, and he wasn't prepared to entertain guests there.

To my faint surprise, Mr. Asherwood was still allowed a kettle and toaster in his rooms, possible because they were the only pieces of kitchen equipment, except for the fridge, that he hadn't manage to irretrievably lose or injure himself upon. While this was supposed to be a "luxury apartment", the unfortunate resemblance to student accommodation remained, this time with one-room bedsits that used an unconvincing MDF partition to make a separate kitchen.

The impression wasn't helped by the room being inhabited by a human jackdaw. The whole point of Asherwood Antiques was Mr. Asherwood trying to sell some of the little trinkets he'd acquired over the years. This had been mostly at the insistence of the late Mrs. Asherwood, a patient woman who had quite understandably wanted to recover her house from the tides of 1920's porcelain.

Clem picked his way over a dozen or so pieces of Clarice Cliff crockery. "Mr. Asherwood, I'm Clem. I'm a friend of Helen."

Mr. Asherwood looked at me, then at Clem. "Who the hell's Helen? Some new girl doctor?"

I kept my face smooth. It's been two years, and I'm still not used to the way he just...goes away. "He means me."

"Ah, Miss Hawthorn!" Mr. Asherwood brightened. "Is it Saturday already?"

I sat down diagonally opposite Mr. Asherwood. "You have many wonderful things here. Do any of them have mercury in them?"

"Quicksilver?" Mr. Asherwood smiled mistily. "I got in awful trouble with that when I was a lad, you know. I had this reddish-brown stone, cinnabar it was called. All my interesting rocks went in the windowsill, and that was a hot summer. You don't get that kind of summer, it's just drought now. Mum was furious, she looked at my cinnabar and there were these little beads of quicksilver on the surface. I could have been poisoned." Mr. Asherwood crumpled, all of a sudden. "Miss Morrisey thinks she's being poisoned, when they give her the tablets. I don't like it here."

Such a simple, heartbreaking thing to say. I couldn't help hugging him. To my surprise, he leaned into the hug.

"Hello, Mum," he said softly.

I looked up at Clem. "Can't you do something for him? Some sort of..." the words 'magic angel healing-fu' sprang to mind, but I was damned if they were springing to tongue as well.

"They get mercy, not miracles." He sighed. "I'm sorry, Helen. If I had the power you think I have, do you think any of you would know a moment's pain?" He took one of the hands I had wrapped round Mr. Asherwood's shoulders. "Mercy is needed, but it's not necessarily...nice."

"Mercy's a strange metal," mumbled Mr. Asherwood. "It's runny, you know. You can float cannonballs in it."

I released him. "Do you have any here?"
"Why yes, Miss Hawthorn, I certainly do." Weakness forgotten, Mr. Asherwood near as dammit bounded over to the chest of drawers by his bed. I didn't want to peek, I guess that sort of thing is private, but there's no telling what Mr. Asherwood accumulated in his lifetime. He probably kept the keys to that restored Hillman he used to drive in the Holy Grail.
With a certain amount of scrabbling, Mr. Asherwood found what he was looking for in the second drawer, and squawked in triumph. "Here we go, Helen! Oooh, let me sit down a minute." He pretty much collapsed on the bed.
Clem and I barged into each other in the rush to help him. Mr. Asherwood was nearly grey, and breathing like a steam engine. "Oh, don't make a fuss, either of you. You're as bad as those white-starched harpies outside. Why do I have this..?"
He held up the item in question. It was a glass disc, six inches in diameter and about an inch thick. Deeply engraved into the disc I saw the cardinal points of the compass, and as it lay flat on the duvet I saw that the movement within was where the glass had been nearly filled with mercury.
Except for the point of the compass. Floating serenely in it's dense pool was a small collection of bones, that had clearly once been-
"First metacarpal, first proximal phalanx, and the first distal phalanx," breathed Clem. "That's my entire thumb! Still attached to each other, I see. But pointing...where?"
I picked up the compass idly, and saw it swing off to the left. Then Clem took a step closer, and suddenly the bone swung round to point at him. Fascinated, I hopped off the bed and circled Clem, watching the bone needle track him flawlessly.
"Good news, Clem. I think this set of bones points to the other bones. You're carrying more of your bones than anything else,

so it defaults to you." My face was reflected in the glass. "This is going to make things a damn sight easier."

Mr. Asherwood looked at us in uncomprehending horror. "Who are you? What are you doing with that? Thieves!"

I opened my mouth to calm him down- and there was a massive explosion.

While Mr. Asherwood and I gaped at each other like startled fish, Clem was already on his feet. "That was out in the living room. Please excuse us, Mr. Asherwood."

"Damn that!" declared Mr. Asherwood, hauling himself upright. "I'm not lying down for thieves and looters! Come along, Helen!"

"Yes, Mr. Asherwood," I replied meekly, sliding the bone compass into my bag. Trotting behind the men, I decided I didn't like the thought of fragile glass in my bag, possibly about to leak mercury, and wrapped the compass with a wedge of tissues.

Outside, the scene was chaos. Little old biddies had been flung all over the living room. It was actually hard to see what the damage was, the nurses coughed into a slowly rising ball of smoke that had once been part of an outer wall.

"Oh, surely not," sighed Clem, for all the world as though somebody had nipped in front of the queue at the post office.

From the still smoking hole in the wall, a shape was emerging, and it took everyone a collective moment to figure out what we were seeing. The figure leaning out of the smoke was an old man, so old and knotted that I though wildly he must have been older than most of the residents. His posture seemed pretty much impossible for something with a normal spine, and his legs didn't seem attached to his hips in the traditional manner. Not that he was using his hips, nor the lower half of his body. His method of locomotion seemed to be effectively a small, horseless chariot.

It was nothing more than a box with three sides removed, and four small wooden wheels. I couldn't hear a motor hidden away, but there seemed to be no other way for the chariot to be propelling itself forward with indomitable grace.

While everyone (yes, including me) gaped at his arrival, and the man produced a small wooden hammer. He tapped the front of his chariot with it, where it came up to his waist. The sound it made was small and hollow, but at that sound door rattled in their frames, and the glass shook in all the windows.

"He's a nephilim," whispered Clem. "No sudden moves, please."

The old man taped his gavel again. "This court is now in session."

"I don't think so," snapped Clem, and suddenly he appeared as I'd first met him, glowing and proudly away from the ground. "I name thee Solomon, and bid three withdraw."

"Clemael." Solomon tried to untwist his arms, and there was a nasty popping of joints. "Over half of these people are steeped in long lifetimes of sin. And don't think I don't know about the Hand of Mercy."

Before anyone could move, he snatched up an old woman, and looked searchingly into her eyes.

"You leave Miss Morrisey alone!" yelled a particularly brave nurse. "She's got Alzheimer's!"

"Solomon!" Clem's voice thundered through the room. "Miss Morrisey is not for you."

"Why not?" In comparison, Solomon sounded a toad croaking under it's rock.

Clem spread his hands in a gesture of understanding. "Because, wisest of judges, she cannot recall her sins. And how can she repent of what she can't recall?"

There was a silence so deep I could hear some of the rubble shifting its own weight.

"I withdraw, then, for now," decided Solomon. "The situation- and my little coz- will be watched. I will not permit the creation of the Hand of Mercy. But these people...they've have lost more or less everything else from their minds. Perhaps it is right that their sins be included in that."

There was no breeze that could have caused the smoke to billow up the way it did, but still it obscured the hole in the wall, and somehow nobody was surprised to find that Solomon had vanished.

"I'm not sure I'm coping with this," I muttered.

"And there are more subtle ways to tell us we are being watched." An entirely human-looking Clem started helping people to their feet, and slightly ashamed, I followed suit, making a point to help Mr. Asherwood. He smiled vacantly at me, and I wasn't sure if he recognised me or not.

"Hello, Mr. Asherwood."

"Ah, Miss Hawthorn. Saturday already?"

Oh, what the hell. I'm no thief, or rather I wasn't then. "Yes, Mr. Asherwood. Um, may I borrow this for a few days?" I showed him the compass.

"That old thing? Jeannie's been telling me to get rid of it for years. The bones scare her, little flower. You keep it."

"Thank you," I said numbly, and tried not to think that Jean Asherwood had been little more than bones herself for about six years now. There were little flowers growing on her grave, daisies and lady's slipper and buttercups and dandelions. Before he became too ill to cope with the wider world, Mr. Asherwood had found that a simple comfort, but a profound one.

Such a terrible thing, to forget daisies.

I stomped away from the main gate of the big house, pleased to put myself as far away as possible from the sight of faded humanity.

"So that's what I've got to look forward to, then." I kicked a stone from the gravel driveway, and was rewarded by a twinge of my knee. Tendons were never meant to fit round without a complete kneecap. "If I'm a good girl, if I don't smoke or drink, if I get my veg and head down the gym, I can expect to end up there."

"Slash your wrists, then," said Clem calmly.

"You what?"

"You're mortal, aren't you? You're going to die soon anyway, so crack on."

I shook my head. "I, no, because...I'm not dead yet. And the bit before I die, that's where I get to live."

Clem smiled in genuine delight, and I felt an odd sensation at the tip of my nose, as though it had just been brushed with a feather.

"Was that...a wing?"

There in front of the main gate, Clem unfolded his wings. I couldn't help staring. It looked as though he'd unfolded them from a place I couldn't see, as though they were always attached to his back, but in a different set of dimensions.

The wings themselves were white, not white like swan's wings, but white like silk. The longer flight feathers, the pinions, looked sturdy enough, but the smallest breeze set them fluttering like scraps of fabric.

I edged closer and closer. Clem had changed his outfit to go with the wings. The sharply-pressed trousers were the same, but instead of the shirt and jacket he had a tunic arrangement. It tightened round his chest strangely (and with the wings, it was clear the chest folded outwards in a way that had less to do

with human musculature and more to do with avian counterbalance), and it occurred to me that the tunic would have to allow for the emergence of wings, so it was probably little more than a series of strategic laces at the back.
"Can you actually, you know, fly? I don't mean floating, I mean..." I burbled into silence.
"Yes." He said it calmly, but I'd heard a lot of Clem's calm tones by then, and I could pick up a tiny hint of the joy he felt flying, soaring through the cold, clean skies of Creation. I smiled at the thought, and he smiled back, one wing curving towards me.
"Would you care to touch it?"
I swear, the eyebrow twitch was just a reflex.
I reached out my right hand, then thought about it, reached out my left. It's not that I thought Clem would deliberately hurt me, but accidents happen, and I'm pretty fragile even by human standards.
The wing was so soft. Even the flight feathers were as soft as down, and the entirely weightless fluff towards the top was so delicate the nerves in my fingertips fired in little prickles, trying to get more information about what I was touching. Fascinated, I swept my hand up to the edge of the wing, tracing the feeling of bone and flesh to the bottom of Clem's shoulder blade.
Clem's utter silence drew me. Eyes closed, not even breathing, but still like a horse expecting the raised whip to fall.
Finding the join between body and wing had brought me close to Clem, close enough to dance with him if I liked. "If you don't like it," I murmured reassuringly, "tell me to stop."
His lips parted in a nearly-unheard "oh," and with a flush I realised that I'd mistaken the problem.
Embarrassed and pitying, I took a step back, and his eyes

opened.

"We should-" his voice was too quiet. "We have the mercury. We should go."

"Yes," I said , and tried not to think of the softness on my fingertips.

Chapter Three

After a night of hot and tangled dreams, I woke up about twenty minutes before my alarm went off. Dozy, I ran my bath with too much cold water, and squealed as I sank into it. Did a good job of waking me up, though, so I grabbed my stick and vaguely wondered, as I did every morning, whether it was time to go to the optician. The view outside my bedroom has been gently blurring for some years now.

To my own faint surprise I managed to get an early bus into town, and rewarded myself by heading down a backstreet bakery for a breakfast Eccles cake. I'm aware that I should probably give my knees less weight to carry, but the way I see it they're screwed anyway, so I might as well get some enjoyment out of life. And food is always the pleasure that has the least in the way of distressing and disgusting bodily fluids.

Unlocking the shop door, I stepped over the bills on the threshold before scooping them up and tutting slightly. Next up was the computer, so I booted that up and waited for it as I counted out the float for the till, before opening a browser and looking up a few things. It was then I realised my eyes had been resting on Clem standing outside the window for ten minutes.

I poked my head out the door. "I don't have to invite you over the threshold, do I?"

"It's not necessary," replied Clem, "but it probably is good manners."

I held the door open for him. "Then I guess I invite you into the shop."

Clem looked around the shop, quietly admiring the stock. "You weren't at your flat today."

"Of course not." I flicked a cloth round the counter. "It's

Monday." I sighed at his expression. "I have a shop to run. Five and half days a week, I'm behind this counter."
Clem stood there, watching with neutral eyes.
I broke under the silence. "This is my shop, pretty much, Started out as the Saturday girl, now I'm the manager. This is my job, you know? You dispense chrisms of mercy, I dispense bits of Victorian tat and Art Deco follies."
"So, it's not an essential service, then." Clem's voice was patient, as though he hoped I'd start to realise my folly before he had to explain it.
"Don't you take that tone with me," I snapped. "This was Mr. Asherwood's dream. I don't know if you get this, but here in the mortal world, we've got to look after each other's dreams."
Clem fetched out a Shaker chair and sat down. "Solomon distressed you. I'm sorry about that."
There was an ancient PC by the till that I normally used for stocktaking. Now I swung the monitor around to face him. "The day before yesterday I didn't have to go search for the definition of what a nephilim is. Took me three goes to spell it, as well. How can you have a human-angel hybrid, anyway?"
"When the first humans walked in creation, it was a little uncertain as to whether they'd flourish or wither. So a set of angels named the Grigori were set over them to watch."
"And they got a bit...involved?"
"Most of them, yes. They were created to be fascinated by humans, and humans tend to be fascinated by angels."
"Yes, well," I burbled. "So their children were the nephilim."
"Exactly. When the pureblood humans settled in new lands, they were shocked to find these deformed, angry giants. Of course, they wouldn't be giants by today's standards. But their bones were twisted and bent, too dense for angels, too fragile for humans." I wondered if Clem realised he was rubbing his

crystal hand. "Those that survived had been rejected by their mothers, and their fathers were not allowed to perceive their existence. So they were rejected, and they were angry, and they were in pain."

"Well, that sucks," I declared. "And Solomon was one of these?"

"King Solomon the Wise, born from Chokkma, angel of wisdom, and king David. He's effectively now the agent of Judgement, my diametric opposite."

"I did think he had a cob on for you," I observed, rifling through the books under the counter. "I hope we don't meet him again next time."

I got out an Ordnance Survey map, and carefully put the compass down on top of it. "All right, Clem, back off. We're going to see if this works."

"Even using a map?" Clem went to run a fastidious finger over a glass display, then stopped when he saw my expression.

"Apparently so." I squinted cautiously at the compass. The bone rotated slowly in its bath of mercury, before settling somewhere to the left of the page.

"West country," I reported, and flipped to the relevant page. "I hope it's Devon, Devon's well nice at this time of year."

Clem watched his own bones swing. "Sorry, that looks like Cornwall. Oh...wait. What was that line about tin?"

I fished the piece of paper out from under the till. It's where I keep all important bits of paper; one of these days I'm just going to lift up the till and tell Inland Revenue to help themselves. "Knockings in the dark."

"I know where we're going," sighed Clem. "Can you drive? I suspect we shall need to borrow a car."

I closed the map, and slid the compass back into my bag. "I'm not going. I'm sorry, Clem, but if I close up the shop we'll lose business, and if I call in one of the casual workers, I'll have to pay them. Either way, I lose money, and this place isn't rich enough to skip a day's takings. I'm sorry."

Clem looked utterly woebegone, and I tidied up some papers on the counter rather than look at him. "It's a terrible thing, to be so enslaved. I'll return to you on Sunday, then. Though we may be away overnight."

"Oh, bloody hell." I sighed. "I can get the Saturday casual in here on her own, that frees up the whole weekend. But I'm not making a habit of this."

"I don't mean to be..." Clem gave me a little neck bow, it made him look like a pigeon in spring. "I'm sorry, Helen."

"Hmph," I mumbled without true anger. "I'll bet I even have to pay the car hire."

"I have nothing to pay with," he agreed.

"Oh, I dunno, There are docks in Bristol, you're quite pretty- oh, your face!" Little giggles racked their way through me.

"I wouldn't be much of a gigolo," said Clem gravely. "I lack such things as would make prostitution possible."

I gaped in a really undignified way. "You don't have..? But, but, nephilim!"

"Procreative metaphysics." Clem's voice softened. "*When spirits embrace, total they mix, union of pure with pure desiring. Nor strained conveyance need, as flesh to mix with flesh*'."

I blinked, recognising the quote. "Paradise Lost, right?"

"Angel sex." Clem rolled his eyes. "You offer a human the secrets of the universe, the wisdom of the divine, and four out of five times they're more interested in whether angels have sex."

I grinned. "We're great like that. If we see a new thing, we want to know if we can kill it. If we can, we then want to know if we can have sex with it, before, during or after. If we can make money of it as well, so much the better!"

"I'm guessing from your tone humanity does not have some sort of opt-out clause, still."

"I'm still looking." I flipped open the phone book, and started flipping through to Car Hire. "Hope my insurance is up to this."

Chapter Four

I'd hired quite a decent Rover for our trip to Cornwall. Clem was mostly silent, watching the landscape as we rolled through. I guess he wasn't used to seeing it go by at ground level.

Really, we should have set off a bit earlier, because by the time we arrived at the tip of Cornwall, it was already mid-afternoon.

I stepped out of the car, and was instantly slapped by the wind. There were cliffs on two sides, and rough grass that would smell of sea salt if I got too close. The place was undeniably bleak, but I think it depended on your mood as whether you found it desolate or beautiful.

The only sign of humans past or present was the rough track we'd driven down, and tall half-ruined buildings with even taller chimneys. The wind whistled through the broken brickwork, and mingled unsteadily with the sound of distant gulls.

I read the warning signs carefully. "Clem, this is starting to sound dangerous. Some of these mines stretch out to under the sea. Are we going to have to go down?"

"Into the depths." Clem's voice was very quiet. "Into the dark, because I have no wish to offer insult down there."

I raised a finger. "You want me to go down a dangerous abandoned mine working that reaches under the sea, with no light source whatsoever, and no hope of rescue if it falls on me or I get trapped or anything. Clem, you're on your own with this one."

"I will protect you. In return for your company." I thought Clem's eyes were a little too wide. It simply hadn't occurred to me that angels could be nervous.

I looked up at the sky. "Oh, bloody hell, Clem. I hope you

brought a rope."

Clem hadn't brought a rope.

"Take both my hands," he instructed, "and close your eyes."

Trying not to swear in front of an angel, I did as I was told. There was a slight pop in my ears, then I felt my shoes land on thin gravel.

"We just floated down," I whispered. The darkness and the silence of the mine reminded, somehow, of the hush in a cathedral. It didn't have that holy quality that the Greeks called 'numinous', but the age and the solidity of the rock around us made me quiet and respectful.

"We can talk," Clem assured me in a low voice, "but we should keep our voices down, there are those who haven't heard a strange voice in a while."

I heard it then, the strain in Clem's tone. "What is it?" I asked as gently as possible.

"I'm being foolish. I just... don't like underground very much. The rock pressing down on me, it flattens me, crushes me away from the sky." I could hear that Clem had started breathing again, a little too fast for normal rest.

"Oh, Clem it's okay, you'll be fine." I reached out to where I thought his voice was coming from, and at the touch of my fingertips brushing his shoulder he palpably flinched.

Silently cursing my clumsiness, I wrapped my arms round him, and heard, of all things, a heartbeat.

"It's okay," I whispered against him, and went to kiss his cheek. But I must have missed, because the kiss landed on the edge of his mouth.

Then he was holding on to me, painfully tightly, the way someone having a nightmare would cling to their pillow. And our lips had found each other despite the utter lack of light, and were even less inclined to part.

Clem let go, suddenly, as though he'd woken suddenly, and I stumbled, not appreciating how much I'd been leaning into him.
"Helen, I'm sorry, I'm so sorry-"
"Feeling better?" I cut across him before he could work himself up into a fine old remorse. My pride wasn't going to stand for someone being mortified that they'd kissed me.
"Yes, I. er..." He coughed, trying to find something to say. "This isn't, it's not the best place I could have brought you, on the whole."
I kicked up some gravel, as quietly as possible.. "It's a bloody mine. I thought these things were all empty of tin now, anyway?"
"Empty of tin," said Clem gravely, "but not the creatures that lived in the mine."
I boggled a bit at this. "What, there's a colony of feral canaries down here?"
He didn't chuckle. "There are the Knockers."
"The what? You'd better tell me, there's no way I'm putting 'knockers' into a search engine."
"Also known as the Bucca, the Coblynau, and in Prussia the Wichtlan. If you leave some food out for them, they knock on the walls to indicate where the rich seams of ore can be found."
Despite the fact that I was being told this by an angel, I found a suitably withering look. "There are fairies at the bottom of the mineshaft?"
Something that sounded like an aggrieved woodpecker started up by my left ear. I felt the air move as Clem turned, and wondered if he was daft enough to be wearing wings in a narrow mine shaft.
"Name yourself, little one."
"Is that Clemael?" The voice in the darkness had a tapping quality. "How does the leg?"

"Oh, that." Clem sounded surprised. "I haven't thought of that in a long time. It healed cleanly, thank you. Is that Salve, then?"

"Why don't you shine a light and find out?" The voice giggled in the darkness.

"If it doesn't offend you," said Clem quietly.

In the light of Clem's glowing (and it occurred to me that the glow was rather more subdued than usual) I found myself looking at what could have passed for a small, ugly child. The knocker was pale, the kind of pale that hasn't seen the sun in centuries, with a vaguely amphibious-looking face that was saved from being completely hideous by the presence of lot of laughter lines round the eyes. There was something wrong with the line of the shoulders, and blinking I saw it was because there were stubs of bone rising from somewhere on Salve's back.

"You're another angel?" I gaped.

"Once were angels." Salve sighed. "Told to heal. Not told who to heal."

"Hmm." Clem's glow flickered. "All right, that's true enough. Come the Fall, the battle was hot and fast, loyal against fallen. The Healers were a fast mash unit, designed to get in there, drag the wounded out of the front lines, and patch them up."

"And so we did."

"Indeed, but they not only saved and healed the loyal, they saved and healed the fallen as well."

"They were our brothers. We could not let them suffer and bleed when we could have saved them."

I pinched the bridge of my nose. "And you got busted down here for it?"

"Too loyal to fall, too fallen to stay. Clemael tried to broker a deal for us to come to Earth."

"Well, that sucks!" I nearly stomped my foot. "All you did was

help people." I had a thought. "If you were angels, that might be why the bone compass brought us here. It's not one Clem's bones at all."
Clem watched Salve's expression a lot more closely than I did. "That's not true, is it? Have you got part of my hand?"
"Reminds us of who we were."
To my surprise, Clem sat down next to Salve. "Can I have it back? Will you help me heal my hand?"
"We aren't angels any more. Now there are rules."
"Rules?" Clem sat there, blinking.
"You're fairies, pretty much," I was thinking aloud, so nearly missed the identical expressions of disapproval. "Fairies don't give stuff away, they...swap it. Is that right?"
I might have imagined it, but Clem flared golden light for a moment before he got control of himself. "Well then. What do you want in exchange for my bones?"
"We want the fire of saint Bridget. Humans make it last twenty days. We can make the light live forever."
I folded my arms, and looked over at Clem. "Quick trip to Ireland then? Hope you can carry passengers, I've lost my passport."
"That's won't be necessary," said Clem.

To my surprise, Salve came with us. He blinked a bit as he took a step, then another.
"Are you sure you want to do this?" Clem was concerned, and wordlessly held a hand out to the smaller ex-angel.
"I miss the light. I might be of help to you. I like helping. The mine is so empty now. One day,the bell rang and our human friends went home. And never came back."
"The tin mines all closed," I said as gently as possible. "Most of the mines in the country, the minerals were all mined out, and

men turned away."

A mixture of emotions crossed Salve's face. "I miss them so much, helped them in the dark. But I hope they are somewhere safer."

I took out a small pad, and after a certain amount of scrabbling in my handbag produced a cracked biro. "I reckon I'd better write down 'Fire of Bridget', for later."

I had a tickly feeling. Sometimes, people in town ask me to value their Mum's old collection plates, and I trot along, only to find three different generations squabbling over who owns the plates, who promised them in which will, and in the middle someone's Mum herself, swinging around her nearest and dearest indiscriminately with an iron, or worse, a solicitor.

In short, my finely honed dealer senses warned me that this was about to get messy.

I showed Salve how to buckle his seatbelt and gave him my woolly coat in case the light got too scary. He blinked nervously, and I wished I owned a pair of sunglasses as well.

The Rover took a couple of times to start, until Clem smiled at the dashboard.

"If you could, please..?"

The engine fired, smooth as burning silk.

I waited until we were safe on the motorway before asking more questions. Clem sat quiet and composed as though in prayer- always a possibility with angels, I suppose- and Salve was trying to figure out how to stick his head out the window despite the seatbelt.

"You'll get decapitated if you do that," I advised him. I sound like my Dad sometimes.

Salve made a face. "Yes, that would hurt for a long while."

I smiled despite myself. "Now, look, I don't mean to insult two such, uh, bastions of monotheism, but the thing about Saint

Bridget is, well, she didn't start out as a saint."
Clem looked across at me. "This is about her being a goddess, isn't it?" For a moment, I felt the swish of distant, immanent wings as he considered his words. "Understand, there has always been the goddess Bridhe-" He pronounced it Breed- "of the Bright Spear, and there's always been Saint Bridget. It's the same person. Just...running in parallel."
I lifted a finger, then lowered it again. "All right, confused. The goddess and the saint are the same, but different?"
"Humans, I think have trouble with this. You're the ones that believe, rather than are believed in. If you're defined by what people believe about you, over time there are contradictions. "
"Like me," piped up Salve, fiddling with the window control. "I'm an angel, a knocker, and a kobold. All at once."
"Different people believe different things in different times and places." I thought about it as I watched the junctions slide by.
"Wow, I'd hate that. I mean, having my whole...nature based on what people think of me."
Clem looked across at me, but didn't say anything.

Apocrypha

In a place that would later be referred to as a garden, four figures stood, about half a foot above the irridescent grass.
Tallest and darkest of the four was Gabriel, currently inspecting the ground beneath him. "If I travel too close to the base clay, these white plants erupt from the grasses."
Michael, broad-shouldered and tanned by newborn stars, seldom looked down. "The man named them lilies. Are they what you designed?"
Everyone's ears pricked up, not entirely metaphorically.
"Designed?" said auburn Sammael, as always managing to sound distracted.
"Word came from the Metatron three... mornings ago." Michael pronounced the unfamiliar word carefully. There had, after all, only been a dozen or so mornings so far. "We may design a creature after our own imagining, and it will be created."
"And you've already chosen yours," said oddly-shaped Chokkma. Something was wrong with Chokkma's voice too, it was light and high, like a thoughtful dove.
"My creature has already been presented to Adam." Michael beamed with pride. "He named it a Lion."
Sammael floated on his back, watching the clouds. "What about you, Gabriel?"
"Well, it won't be lilies," chuckled Gabriel.
Sammael turned onto his stomach, and the smile he turned on Chokkma was that of a predator. "I think I shall ask for something subtle. Let there be stubby little limbs, but a long, sinous body, covered in protective scales. And he shall be intelligent, and softly spoken. What do you think, Chok?"

Chokkma forced the panic down in her stomach. How did Sammael know? How could he? "It sounds well enough," she said as casually as possible. "But my creation- that is, my creature- is more subtle still."

Both Gabriel and Michael frowned, and she smiled at their expressions. "Brothers, haven't you noticed I have the same shape as the woman Lilith? She was my idea."

"Oh!" Michael blurted. "I did wonder why you'd been created that way. It was obviously meant to inspire you."

"Yes." Chokkma smiled thinly. "Even the shape of my hips is meant to manipulate me."

Sammael frowned for a moment, but said nothing.

Chapter Five

By the time we got back to my flat, it was dark. I parked the Rover under a street light, I wasn't sure if that made it more secure or less, I just knew I was tired and aching and wanted it to stop for the night. I stilled the engine, and rubbed my legs unhappily.
Salve watched me with a professional interest. "Both knees?"
"Yep." I leaned on my stick as I got out the car. "the patella, that's the kneecap, is pretty much talcum power, the ends of the femur and tibia are corroding faster than an operation would be able to replace."
"Why?"
I decided not to voice my suspicions. "Something my Mum had passed down to me. She died of it, when I was a baby. Though it was way worse in her case, a sort of massive calcium meltdown."
"Patellar resurfacing of any use to you?"
So he'd kept up with human medicine. I wasn't entirely surprised, though I couldn't help wondering if some Cornishman was still dropping medical journals down the old chimneys.
"There's not really enough left to resurface. I hate it when they take the x ray, and the osteopath does that little sucking-in-breath thing."
"I'm sorry for that," decided Salve after an appropriately sombre pause. "What about anti-inflammatory drugs?"
"They don't really help." I fidgeted awkwardly. I think about my knees way too much of the time, talking about them aloud seemed an even worse version of that. "I just take painkillers half an hour before bed."

"Leave me a pasty out tonight," advised Salve, "and you can skip the painkillers."

I ran through a mental inventory of my fridge. "I've no pasties, what's the view on a scotch egg?"

"Once more do I martyr myself before my calling." Salve sighed, slightly theatrically.

"Close enough," I sighed.

I'd expected the shrine of a saint, or indeed a goddess, to be somewhere remote and windswept, with a small chapel or maybe even standing stones.

I didn't expect it to be in someone's garage.

In a row of semi-detached houses in a sleepy suburb, Clem and I picked our way past expensive cars and tiny gravel lawns with larger pebbles studded here and there, like really uptight Zen gardens. All the barrenness, none of the tranquillity.

The first things I noticed was the BMW sitting on the narrow road, rather than pampered in some garage. The second thing I noticed was that while most of the houses had sturdy fake-stone walls, this one had several panels of dark wrought iron spikes, in several different styles. And unlike the low wooden gates on their creaking hinges, This one had iron gates a good six feet in height.

I rubbed my nose, considering matters. "Two questions. Why couldn't we bring Salve, and did anyone bring a stalk of fennel?"

"Perhaps we could trade for a coal from the flames. And Salve is still adjusting to the world above ground."

From inside the garage came the sound of constructive hammering.

"Sounds like a smithy in there," I observed, opening the gate. Oiled hinges, I noticed. "I'd better knock, you look like you're going to peddle some crackpot religion."

Clem flashed me a smile. "Wouldn't be the first time, by any means."

I couldn't imagine what I was going to say. But that doesn't usually stop me, so I knocked on the garage door.

There was a pause, and then a woman in greasy jeans and heavy gloves opened a small side door. A waft of oily heat accompanied her, and I was pleased her garage was detached from the house, if only for the sake of fire hazards.

In my peripheral vision, I saw a second figure step out from behind the garage, and my neck prickled. I hoped I wasn't being deliberately outflanked, especially since I had no idea where Clem had got to.

"Hi there," said the woman. "Can I help you?"

"Um, yes." I decided to go for broke. "Um, I appear to be on the world's oddest scavenger hunt. Could I have a coal or bit of wood or something from your forge, please?"

The woman raised her voice. "What do you reckon, Poet?"

"You get inside, Birch. That commission isn't going to make itself."

"Nor does it need making in the next ten minutes." Birch winked cheerfully at me, and Poet smiled ruefully.

"Okay, you two are both being really nice about this. Um, is it okay if I go ahead and help myself?"

"It's not that easy," sighed Poet. "The fire is just coal and stuff. It's lost its other properties."

I sagged visibly. "Dammit. So it goes out like normal?"

Man and woman looked at me curiously. "That's one hell of a scavenger hunt. Do you want to come in?"

Poet and Birch made a very decent mug of green tea. I do like green tea, I feel all clean and healthy for drinking it.

"So go on, then," said Birch, stretching in her jeans. "Who set you hunting? I mean, you look pretty human."

I decided not to mention Clem, I wasn't sure why he'd made himself scarce, but that probably meant he didn't want to be noticed, much less talked about. "I owe a bit of a favour to the knockers in the tin mines of Cornwall. They live in darkness all the time, you see, and ever since the mines closed, they've been cold and sad."

Poet retied his hair. "Well, you're a bit stuffed. Mostly, we make wrought iron stuff, yeah? There's not much call for a trained farrier round here, so the gates and stuff, that's okay. But then, then we had to dabble in religion."

"It's not dabbling," muttered Birch, and I had the feeling this was an old argument that didn't really need reheating.

"Anyway... we made a lance. Solid gold, a few other holy bits and bobs as offerings, and presented it to what we thought was an avatar of Bridget. Turns out when we gave it away, it took the goodness out of our fire."

"We can still do iron," Birch chipped in, "but it's costing us a fortune in fuel."

I leaned on my stick, considering. "Okay then. I find this golden lance, give it back to you, you then magic up your fire, you then give me a bit of that fire that I can then take to Cornwall, and sort out the knockers. Does that sound okay?"

"Just power up the fire, that's all we're asking." Poet topped up my cup. "Deal?"

I let the green tea feeling spread through me. "Deal."

Birch smiled. "Good hunting."

I wasn't surprised to find Clem already in the car. He looked up from the paper Nana Sophie gave me, smiling faintly. "What's another name for a lance?"

"A spear- oh wait, they did say it was solid gold." I rubbed my eyes. "Where the hell are we going to find a fake avatar of Bridget?"
"You mean Roisin Gallagher?" Clem had more than one piece of paper on his lap. "While you took tea and cake, I took a good look around the forge. They had this news clipping in the bottom drawer."
I cast an eye over it dubiously. "This a newspaper ad. Probably one those back-page ones you find in the Sunday supplements." From what I could tell from the small and grainy photo, Roisin was a woman much attached to paisley scarves, and a low cut top speckled at the front with assorted talismans.

```
LET ROISIN O'BRIDGET CHANGE YOUR LIFE!
Using ancient techniques from the green
   hills of IRELAND to to HEAL you, to
 bring LOVE into your life, or to help
      you with your MONEY worries.
```

I checked the phone number, placed next to the name R.B. Gallagher.
"If Birch and Poet possessed a working number for Roisin," observed Clem, "They would have the lance back by now."
I shrugged. "It's enough to put into a search engine."
Which is exactly what I did.

Roisin was depressingly easy to find,if you knew what you were looking for. Bridget Gallagher, as she now was calling herself, no longer offered up her vague services through newspapers, but had a website resplendent with twirling animated images.
"What's it all for?" Clem was watching a fairy wave a sparkly

wand with the look of a man fighting off a headache.

"I'm not sure- oh, God, that Burning Times GIF is so very late nineties. There seems to be a Wicca 101 page- the sort of thing that makes me feel terribly sorry for Wiccans, frankly. I can't think everyone wants to be known by this healing crystal unicorn bollocks."

Clem smiled. "So, it's just me enjoying the neopagan revival? It's starting to feel like a school reunion out there, only we're all really, really successful."

"Nana Sophie wanted to raise me- well, Gnostic, actually, but Dad put his foot down, so I'm a really nosy C of E."

Clem laughed aloud. "I'm not at all surprised!"

I stuck my tongue out at him- then blinked. "At last, the website-y money shot. Turns out our Roisin runs a psychic museum."

"Hmm." I tapped my chin thoughtfully. "What's the quickest and easiest way of doing this?"

"We could buy the lance?" Clem read the page over my shoulder.

"It's solid gold, Clem. There's no way in hell I could afford it. And I'm not going on a fund-raiser, I'm on the side quest of a side quest as it is. I wonder how cynical Roisin is?"

Chapter Six

Within ten seconds of stepping into the museum, I realised I knew quite a lot of Roisins.
Every so often, through house clearance or little local auctions, I get hold of antique thimbles. And when I do, i's all I can do not to cackle with glee, because that sort thing has plenty of collectors. Middle-aged women, mostly, though there are a few men. They believed that they are absolutely entitled, in a way that makes the divine right of kings seem like a child's preference for strawberry ice cream over chocolate chip, that they should own every thimble they lay their eyes on, never mind the price, the authenticity, or frankly the beauty of the piece. Sometimes if my knees are giving me gyp I'll play the game, let them think they're haggling me out of business, when the final price is a lot higher than the bargain price I paid. They just collect, with fiery determination but little actual joy in what they have. Once it's safely on the shelf or in the cabinet, I swear half these collectors stop caring.
Roisin Gallagher fitted this mould perfectly.
She'd refined her wardrobe since her newspaper days. Now her hair was tied back with little plaits confining the main mass, and I was pretty sure I caught a glimpse of glitter when she moved her head. Her lipstick wasn't actually black, but it was a dark enough brown to bring her complexion into stark whiteness, which the severe black dress did nothing to change.
The museum was laid out in a similar way, actually. The whole city was medieval in a deeply tourist sort of way, Roisin had simply bought a large shop at the end of yet another cobbled alley, and turned it into a gauzy, monochrome haunted house.
"Oh, my life." I looked at the façade. "She's stuck that MDF

sign directly onto the sixteenth century beams. Kill her for me, please."

Clem shook his head. "Mercy, remember?"

"That's just an excuse not to do anything." This sort of thing made me itch, and I wasn't sure why. When did I turn from being a girl working in an antiques shop to being an antiques dealer?

To my surprise, Roisin herself was serving in the ticket booth.

"Good morning. Would you like a full tour, the half tour, or the Darkness tour with the Crowley exhibition? Over eighteens only on that one." The words were friendly, but her tone was distinctly bored.

"Two adults for the full tour, please." I smiled winningly. Well, there were teeth showing.

Roisin named a price that made me grimace. I thought I'd had enough cash in my purse, but clearly this was a job for the debit card.

Clem kept looking round with polite interest. I like the idea of the good trying to look normal while the normal tried to look evil. Not that Roisin would admit that was what she was doing, she'd probably get quite indignant in fact.

Clutching our tickets (and already dreading our inevitable stroll through a gift shop or two), Clem and I set off into the first exhibition.

I think I was expecting a fairground ride, glow-in-the-dark skeletons popping out if boxes to a soundtrack of "woo" noises. Instead, I was plunged into a dark room, the constellations picked out on the ceiling and upper walls in tiny lights.

"Woah," I said faintly.

"Makes you want to soar through the spaces between the light, doesn't it?" Clem looked up as though longing to take off.

I looked down quickly at first, in case the lights were going to hypnotise me or something. Clem was wearing shiny black dress shoes,that looked as though they'd never known a moment of dust or mud.

"Aries then Taurus..." he muttered. "I think it's the way they lead to to the door."

I chanced a quick glance. "Then the door will be near Pisces. Shall we?"

Pretty, glittery things, however astronomically correct, were starting to wind me up, so I gratefully stepped under two interlocked fish and went into the next room.

It was warmer than it should have been. Considering the room was made to be a cave of stone. Not polystyrene, or plaster, or even concrete, no, I'm talking dressed stone. Welsh slate underfoot, if I was any judge, and then once I got my antiques eye in the smaller pebbles along the side of the path could have been polished coal, the larger stones some heavy grey slabs that made me think, oddly, of Edinburgh. The cave effect made a pseudo-natural corridor, and I wasn't surprised to feel a slight pressure on my sleeve as Clem grabbed my arm without making it obvious he was nervous.

"I don't understand." His voice was steady. "I see the gallery, but where are the exhibits?"

I looked around, but didn't really keep track of my surroundings. "They're here,I think. These wall-rocks could be hollow, or it could be all about the interesting minerals... Did I pay for the full tour or the half tour?"

Clem glanced at the perforated card in his hand. "Full tour."

I tapped his hand, then put a finger to my lips. It occurred to me that if the exhibits were hidden in the rock, what else could be hidden? CCTV was pretty much a certainty, and maybe a door... I had a vision for Roisin appearing like a pantomime demon.

"What's the little jewels running down the side there?" Clem's voice was light, casual, and sounded less suspicious than silence would have.

"It's, oh, I know this one! It's bluejohn. It's found in Derbyshire and all round there." I was a little bit pleased with myself for that.

"They're not particularly blue." Clem leaned closer and discreetly drew an arrow symbol over the pattern of bluejohn embedded in an otherwise unremarkable piece of igneous rock. I got the idea- like Pisces, the things were a guide to get to the next room. But why would we need a guide to figure out how to travel a corridor with no other obvious openings? Maybe the corridor was different each time you went down it, or maybe it was the same but opened out into a different place.

I took Clem's hand, and he raised no protest.

"Bluejohn isn't, I mean, it is sort of blue-ish. But the French decided it's more blue-and-yellow. Bleu-jaune, you see?"

There was a distant trickle of water, and a solid hole of light up ahead. Looking round, I realised that the tunnel was lit by recessed cups carved into the rock, containing little electric candles.

"Oh," I heard myself say faintly, "I don't want to go into the light. Knowing my luck it's an oncoming train."

Clem smiled, "Then let's tear up the rails."

I blinked at him, surprised by the martial turn. Thinking about it though, angel's weren't all about the pretty, where they? Flaming sword in hand, Clem had probably chalked up more wartime flight hours than the entire RAF.

The thought carried my feet all the way out of the cavernous corridor.

The room was- what, blue, green? The light, now that we were in it, rippled, the effects of lights under six inches of achingly pure water. Clem and I were standing on a bridge that was nearly invisible, just over the surface of the water that I was prepared to bet was toughened glass. Behind us, out of my peripheral vision, was a trickling sound apparently designed to act upon any human brain and turn it into contented relaxed mush. I suspected it probably had a similar effect on a lot of human bladders.

"We've got this wrong," muttered Clem, his lips barely moving. I made a low inquisitive noise.

"This isn't a museum." Clem let go of my hand. "It's a preserve."

"Strawberry or ras-"

I saw it then. One of the underlit ripples was moving in the wrong direction. Come to think of it, why was the water rippling incessantly at all, with no wind?

No wonder I'd been jumpy, and I was sort of grateful for the realisation that I wasn't just being paranoid. There were things, creatures I couldn't see but my hindbrain still noticed.

On the whole, I would have preferred cameras.

Clem took my hand, and for a moment I almost smiled before he flipped it palm uppermost and started writing letter on my palm with his finger.

The touch of him on all those sensitive nerve endings made me shiver slightly, eyes trying to close. As I result, I missed the first letter entirely, and only got the next letters as a result of mammoth concentration.

L
E
M
E

I mouthed the word "Elemental?"
He nodded.

I racked my brain. What were water elementals? Mermaids? Hippoc- no, wait, undines. That was it. The water was actually thick with undines, I pictured them all thrashing around, nearly invisible like a writhing mass of stinging jellyfish. It was my turn to grab Clem's sleeve, suddenly sickened.

And that meant...back in the corridor. I turned around, and saw that I was right about the trickle of water. It ran, glistening over the thin slit of earth that formed the end of the corridor. And emerging at an awkward angle, from above the entrance until it trailed delicate leaves into the water, was a gnarled but still aesthetically pleasing willow tree.

I turned all the way round, and groaned. "It's all a womping great big birth metaphor, isn't it?"

Clem took a few more steps over the bridge, nodding politely to the populated water below. "Did it involve a a big cloud or two or raw firmament? I've never experienced birth the messy way. I sometimes wonder if it was the intellectual curiosity in conception and birth that contributed to nephilim."

"We're abandoning subtlety then?" I gave him a sideways look.

This close to the door, the water ripple from a more prosaic source: the breeze ruffling through my hair.

"Air next?" I mouthed at Clem. On the one hand, I'd been expecting a more logical order- Earth, Air, Fire Water was traditional, wasn't it?- but Roisin seemed to working through some sort of human life metaphor. A slightly grumply thought about pretension carried me through into the next room.

I nearly died.

I was on the very top of a mountain. The wind was terrible here, buffeted by the weightless mass of trapped elementals. A certain amount of mental prodding told me they were called sylphs. Now I had the trick of it, I couldn't see them by looking at them directly, but from the corner of my eye I caught glimpses of ever-moving colour.

Looking upwards, I had to appreciate the painting. The whole room, ceiling, floor, and walls, was a three dimensional artwork of gorgeous colours and false perspective. The clouds above were painted sliding into a sunset, so they ranged from fluffy white cumulus under a sturdy blue sky, all around to gold-edged wisps against a sky that had paled to yellow and then at the very horizon, a deeper red.

"It's leading towards fire," I noted, then took a step, and stopped.

A wave of vertigo hit me. Like the water room, there was a bridge, but this bridge was simply made out of three length of ropes lashed inexpertly together, meeting on the other side of the room to help the illusion of distance.

"Oh, my knees are going to hate me," I whimpered.

Clem seemed perfectly at ease. I suppose there's no need to fear heights when you're packing a twelve-foot wingspan. Testing his footing carefully, he drifted over the ropes, and then stepped onto something I couldn't see. I might have thought he was floating, but the soles of his feet landed with an audible click.

"Another glass bridge," he reported cheerfully. "The danger is illusory. You would be best to step between the gaps in the ropes."

I sat gingerly on the platform, then reached a foot carefully between the ropes. Sure enough, about an inch below the bottom rope, my foot felt a solid surface. Further probing revealed that the glass platform was actually wider than the water bridge had been. Pleased, I repeated the process with the other foot, to the same result. It wasn't the most dignified walk ever, but steadying myself on the upper two ropes helped somewhat.

Several steps ahead of me, Clem was tangling his fingers into

nothing, and I wondered if perhaps he was petting the sylphs.
"Why don't they go outside?" I asked.
Clem didn't look at me. "They're trapped here. If you look in the shapes in the clouds, I suspect you'll find certain sigils."
Despite my rope-hampered shuffle, I tried to stand upright. "That's horrible! These things don't seem very dangerous, you wouldn't put paying customers through them if they were. And they're completely packed in, it's like battery animals. How can we get them past the sigils?"
I felt little appreciative breaths against my skin, and Clem smiled. "Elementals are like all animals in that respect, they'll do you no harm if you do no harm to them. Though salamanders are nuisances for getting into the walls of houses."
I took a deep breath, testing out my idea. "What if they were carried away in something?"
He broke into a heart-achingly beautiful smile. "If they were invited, perhaps. Be careful."
I coughed, nervously, made sure I was standing carefully. "I invite as many sylphs are my lungs can safely contain to enter into my lungs until we're outside this building."
I took a deep, filling breath, keeping my shoulder low like an opera singer, trying to take in as much air as possible. I couldn't feel the sylphs go in, and I was pleased for that, because something that felt like an object in my airways would have made me panic. Clem watched from a safe distance, wide-eyed and wondering as he watched bright winds circling me.
Eventually I thought I'd better exhale, though I was slightly worried about dislodging any sylphs near the top. It didn't seem noticeably unpleasant, so I tried to make myself breath normally. It worked, until a sudden stab of headache made me nearly stumble. Clem caught me with an arm round my waist.
"Helen?" He voice was clear in my ear. "Are you feeling

sleepy?"

"Yeah," I muttered, suddenly dozy, "it's making me a bit confused."

He pretty much had to hold me upright, before looking intently at my chest. I've had men stare at my boobs before, of course, but none of them ever then said "Less oxygen, please."

The confusion subsided, though the headache remained a distant pain. "What did they do?"

Clem maintained a hold on my arm. "I think they were trying to be helpful. Offering you plenty of oxygen to help you get through. Another sixteen hours, your lungs would have started to fill with blood."

I didn't have an intelligent response to that.

Conscious of my over-helpful cargo, now stirring lightly in the tiny alveoli of my lung, I half-dragged Clem to the door. It was actually a lot closer than I realised, the foreshortened perspective fooling my sense of distance very effectively.

"It's gilded," said Clem quietly, "but it's still a cage for all that."

"What are fire elementals called?" I asked with my hand on the door.

"Salamanders," Clem advised me. "You might be able to store a couple in your heart, but I really wouldn't recommend it."

"Serious heartburn?"

"Yes, indeed. And your sylph passengers might get consumed."

I'd only had them aboard for a couple of minutes, but it was easy to get protective of little lives sheltering inside me. Patting my ribs reassuringly, I was sure they rewarded me with happy little puffs.

Stepping through that last door was a trial, in many ways.

As I'd suspected, this was the room of fire. Leaving the room of air, my chest clamped as the sigils tried to bind me, but a moment's effort took me through to a place of massive gas jets of flame. The fire was spilling out as though it was an Italian water fountain, spouts of fire, bowls of fire, falls of fire. Some of the bowls contained wood and coal rather than gas, if the crackling sounds were real, and not just a counterpoint to the whoosh of gas.

My eyes started upwards. There was a lot of fire here, and the last thing I was up for was smoke inhalation, or any more subtle dalliances with carbon monoxide. Discreetly placed were ventilation shafts in the ceiling, great slitted chimneys to let the smoke escape.

"Look at me!"

A bank of jets whooshed up, some spitting sparks. When they subsided, a masked figure was standing there like an ancient goddess of vengeance, one finger pointed at the space where Clem and I stood a little past the door.

I kept my breathing shallow, the sylphs inside me churning with rage and fear. "Don't fancy your carbon footprint much, Roisin," I wheezed. "And while the mask is very scary, I've got a skirt just like that. Sort of takes the edge off, you know?"

I felt Clem's hand on the small of my back, supporting me, and I tried not to lean into him.

Beneath the mask, Roisin blinked a bit obviously. "Give me the sylphs. They're mine."

Clem spoke up, not looking at either of us. "Very well, I'll enter into an agreement."

"Clem, you can't!" I yelped.

"Sure he can!" cried Roisin, a faint accent creeping into her vowels. "What do you want?"

Clem turned to face Roisin. He was perfectly grace, perfect gentlemanly elegance. She was a grubby thieving mortal in a mask. "I do apologise. I wasn't speaking to you."

The fires went out.

There was little other illumination, except for the pale slats of daylight above us. The room kept its ambient temperature, which was boiling, but I felt a shudder work through me. The walls, covered in some light red fabric that flapped as though in a thermal, stilled. And there, on the wall behind Roisin, pointing directly to the door below it, was the golden lance. A single, long bone was set and gilded to form a modest cross guard between blade and handle.

"Third metacarpal," said Clem with some satisfaction "I will set free whosoever brings me that bone intact."

"Be clever, Roisin," I advised when I saw her twitch. She looked from Clem to me and back again, and subsided.

Those fires that had been held in coal or wood started smouldering again, sullen red glows deep inside their bowls. The pattern of bowls formed almost landing lights to the spear.

"A co-operative effort." Clem nodded his approval. "Then I'll undertake to free this whole room."

To my surprise the salamanders answered with an audible scuttling noise, before a single, source less flame licked hungrily up at the lance. It had been fastened to the wall by parcel string, of all things, and the salamanders lost no time in burning through the fibres and letting the lance drop to the floor.

Under Roisin's simmering, silent rage, Clem strolled ahead- strolled, mark you- and plucked at the cross guard of the lance. The gold had already been soft, and further heated by the salamander's attentions it parted from the bone easily enough.

Roisin took off her mask. "In return for my co-operation, I ask amnesty."

"You what?" I took three steps towards her.

She didn't flinch, got to give her that. "Your friend there is unravelling the chain of sigils. If those elementals get loose, you'll find me in the paper tomorrow. My heart burnt to ash, my guts full of stones, my lungs an empty vacuum, and my body bloated to the size of Dublin."

Clem and I exchanged a glance. "Lovely mental image, there," I said shakily. "Clem, you mercy her on up, I'll start helping the salamanders."

I picked up a big bowl of smouldering coals, noticing that Clem was scraping away at the far door with the blade of the lance. The bowl was plate-metal, probably a tin alloy, and I wondered if it was my antique skills that told me that, or if this hunt for cardinal metals was finally starting to get to me. At any rate, the bowl was full, and should have been heavy, but it was as light as tissue paper. Odd that the fire elementals should be less destructively helpful than the air elementals.

"All sigils down," reported Clem, with a definite tone of delight. "Madam, you get a twelve hour head start. Use it wisely."

I didn't look up at the drumming of impractical heels, but truthfully I wasn't too worried about Roisin. This wasn't the first time she'd reinvented herself in a hurry, after all. She'd run for a bit, then she'd fortify, if I was any judge, and the beautiful, intricate prison she'd constructed for her elementals suggested I might be.

The bowl was suddenly heavy as lead, and my chest suddenly clenched. I fell forwards in an undignified heap, knees screaming, and lay flat.

"Oh dear," said Clem mildly.

It wasn't wind, or not just wind, at any rate. Even flat on the floor my arse was sufficiently high (and at that point, I rather wished the rest of me was), so that I felt the punching wall of force battering it's way to freedom.

Straight at Clem.

"Down!" I shrieked, understanding the message the elementals tried to convey to me.
Straight into Clem.
He tried not to flinch, but the sheer pressure of a thousand newly-free elementals made his shirt ruffle, then his hair, then his wings folded into view. I thought he was going to use them to shield himself, and for a moment I was worried about his feathers. Then I saw he couldn't even bring them to bear, his wings soared out behind him as though he was flying in place.
Still clutching the bowl, I started edging along the floor towards him.
After a couple of agonising flappings of my knees, it became clear this was a really bad idea. I closed my eyes, and thought some choice words before sliding the bowl in front of me, and dragging myself along by the elbows.
"Welcome to the HMS Helen," I muttered to the sylphs, who by now must have been entertaining some serious doubts. "The rudders are knackered, but at least you don't have to scrub the decks."
"For which, we are all grateful." Clem bent down, and took my hands. "Well, that was bracing. Remind me to get pummelled more often."
I managed to sit up. "Carry the bowl for me please. I see your pummel, and raise you mild oxygen toxicity, and being unable to so much as stand up without my stick."
Both bowl and stick were retrieved, Clem helping me up and leaning me against a wall into the bargain. Turned out the red fabric was actually real silk. No expense had been spared, apparently, and I hoped Roisin had left herself enough of a nest egg to run.
"I wonder how much more of the museum we have left to go through? We did pay for the full tour, after all, and there's any

number of antique exhibits to pique your interest."

"You're kidding," I sighed.

"Indeed I am," laughed Clem. "That's why I propped you up onto the fire escape."

My response made him laugh more. "Why, Helen, I didn't know you could swear in Enochian!"

Chapter Seven

I woke up next morning, knowing two things solidly.
One, there was no way in hell I could put weight on my knees today.
Two, I had no memory of where the hire car was.
 I raised my head, about to fumble around for some serious painkillers, when a noise made me stop. It was humming. In my kitchen. I mentally awarded my burglar ten points for enthusiasm, then deducted them for lack of stealth before my memory finally kicked in.
Oh, wait, that was Salve. I made myself sit up, noting with amusement that someone had basically jammed my nightie on over my day clothes. Nice of the boys not to take advantage, though sleeping in my bra made me feel a little confined about the chest. Unless that was a sylph that had gotten comfy, I had the distinct, unprovable impression that one or two remained beyond the terms of the original invitation.
Salve even knocked on my bedroom door, bless him. "Are you awake?"
"Yes," I said faintly. "Can you grab me a glass of water, please?"
Painkillers in bed, I felt terribly decadent. Sometimes, getting up to get the tablets is what gets me going in the morning. Sundays aside, I can't stay in bed, however bad it's hurting. It's partly due to the shop, of course, but the plain fact is I hurt every morning, and all through the day. Even if I have the best excuse in the world to stay in bed and pull the covers over me, I don't dare. Because if you give up one day, it's way easier to give up the next day, with an excuse that's nearly as good, then to give up the next day, and all the days ever after.

On the other hand, getting up and making my way to the kitchen on bad days like these involved a certain amount of snuffly crying, whimpering, and other things I just didn't want another person to see, not even someone who'd once been a healer among angels.

"Salve," I called, "can you drive?"

Salve near as dammit bounced up and down at the prospect, a worrying sign in itself. "Clem showed me some of the simpler ideas last night. I wouldn't like to try it on a long journey, though."

The thought made me flinch. Where had my brain gone between now and then? "If we brought the hire car back, could you go and check on it, please?"

That little, wrinkly face looked at me with understanding. "I'll have a slow walk over to it, shall I?"

"Thanks," I smiled gratefully, then counted to five, and started the unpleasant task of getting out of bed, on behalf of the next six days.

I dithered what to do until mid week, when I took the bowl of fire and loaded into the hire car. "Listen, guys," I told the salamanders, cheerfully, "I'm taking you to a place where you can be free, and where good people will look after you. They're priests and poets and metalsmiths, you'll be all right there. Anyway, if you stayed at my flat Salve would have ended up sticking a kettle on your heads."

Little licks of flame appeared to laugh at me, and I found myself wishing I could pet salamanders. Sometimes my breath hitched, and that gave me the sneaky confirmation that a sylph really was still nestling in my lung, but it was no bother, and having it felt as though I had protected and contented a vulnerable creature. Score one for my karma.

I put a seatbelt on the bowl as we inched along the M25, firstly out of a badly formed idea of passenger safety, but secondly because the little buggers kept trying to get into the copper wiring of the car. No vet's surgery I could think of would stock those leaflets about caring for your pet when the pet in question was an elemental, but I'd seen Salve coax them away from the electrics with a copper pipe filled with rock salt, so I taped one to the seatbelt, and happy little semi-visible lizards pottered all over it.

When did my life get so strange?

At about five miles out, I fumbled uncertainly with my hand-free kit, and wished I'd typed Birch and Poet's number in before the journey. A spectacularly red-loving traffic light meant that I didn't actually kill anyone, or myself, as I read the number off a sticky note.

"Birchtree Foundries."

"Hi, this is Helen. I've got good news and bad news."

"The Scavenger?" Birch sounded a lot more interested.

"I'm about ten minutes out, I'll let you know when I get there. You might want to lay out some fresh coal on your fire, though."

Birch didn't exactly squeal with glee, but it was close. "I'll have the kettle on."

Poet was waiting for me at the gate, before leading me into her kitchen. "Busy week, huh?"

"You have no idea." I was rather heavier on my stick than usual. "I've got good news, and I've got bad news."

Birch was making the green tea this time, there was no sign of Poet. She took out one of those tea strainers that look like two teaspoons with holes in, and pointed at me as though it was a microphone. "Bad news me."

I passed her a plain holdall. "The spear's busted. No bone, no

virtue, just a big lump of gold."
Birch unzipped the main compartment of the holdall, and with a sound of heavy metal clanking, produced the blade. "Guess I should thank you for bringing the blade. I guess you did your part of the bargain."
I held up a hand. "Actually, the bargain was that I bring power back to your fire, wasn't it? Hence the rather nice bowl I've got here."
Birch looked into the bowl. "Oh, thank you! Hey there, little guys. Damn, Poet's going to kill me for getting more pets."
I laughed. "They're more of an accelerant, really."
She let a single salamander creep over her finger, and I saw it was because she was wearing a copper ring. For a moment, the light on that copper sheen gave me a stab of headache, and she had to repeat her question.
"Are they devas, then?"
I looked up with a small smile. "Well, they're a bit impressed with themselves, but-"
"Not divas, devas!" Birch nearly dropped the bowl in a fit of giggles. "You know, nature spirits."
"Oh, uh, I don't know about that, they're fire elementals, salamanders."
Suddenly all energy, Birch abandoned any pretence at tea, much to my disappointment. "Let's go get them settled in."
The garage was much as I remembered, except that the fire was out. Still, the ambient heat and closeness of the confined space made me wish I'd worn a thinner top, though it did seem to help my knees a little.
"Right, we have coal, newspaper, straw- oh, I've got some wood in the back." Birch was laying down a fire as though participating in a Japanese tea ceremony. "The trick is to make it burn hot, but no so hot that you use up all the fuel too soon."

I looked around with faint curiosity. There was a pair of old fashioned barrels to the side of a forge. One seemed to be filled with oil, probably olive oil from the way the scent raised near-subliminal memories of stirfry. A whole barrel of olive oil, how much must that have cost?

The second barrel smelled briny, and when I nudged it with my toe the surface rippled in a prosaically watery fashion. I figured it was just salt water, which was odd considering there was a trough of water next to the forge.

"Here we go." Birch finished her ministrations, then noticed my investigations. "Impressed yet? Between me and Poet, there's not a lot we don't know about iron and how they used to smith it."

I guess she must have dropped a match into her lovingly assembled fire heap, but all I saw was a gesture before a tiny flame took hold among the newspaper.

Birch nodded at a job well done. "Let's get our new guests in there. Want to do the honours?"

In the end, we took either side of the bowl and then tipped it on a count of three. The little round coals rolled and bounced over to their brethren, and for a moment we could actually hear the salamanders gleefully exploring their new home. It sounded like the crack of badly seasoned seasoned wood, and the sizzle of oil.

The two of us swapped little relieved smiles. "I love a happy ending," said Birch.

I thought of all the bones left to find. "Still waiting for mine. Now, may I have some fire, please?"

Chapter Eight

The difference between salamander-infused flames and the official Fire of Bridget rather escaped me, but I was damn sure the knockers would know the difference, so I took no chances. At any rate, Birch provided me with a massive lantern, which stank of paraffin, and only after much praying over it. I didn't make out any of the words, but the soft cadence she used made me think it was a poem, or at any rate a prayer with rhyming couplets. I wasn't sure if this was such a wonderful idea in a mine probably full of explosive gases, but this was the final part of the deal, and I was so tired of this deal.

There'd obviously been storms since Salve left, though I seriously doubted there was a causal link. The faithful old hire car had put up with a lot of crap from me- I had visions of it sitting on the hire company's lot, bitching to the limo about my clutch control- but when the road ran out of tarmac and became gravel, and moreover gravel with a hell of a lot of fallen masonry all over it, I took pity and killed the engine.

With the car ticking slightly as its components cooled, I looked out over the utter lack of, well, anything. There was probably a cliff nearby, but unless it was about five paces away I'd never spot it until it was too late.

Tutting at my own nerves, I took up the lantern, still burning away merrily, and slung a length of rope over my shoulder. Rope and a lantern; distant memories of watching my first boyfriend play with twenty-sided dice told me that I was now ready for anything, up to and including a multi-level dungeon crawl.

Stepping into the dark, I found I was raising my chin in the unconscious challenge of primates everywhere. Come on then,

I silently dared the night, give it your best shot.
And that's when, over the distant smell of the sea, I caught the scent of fruit.
Not the orchard smell of apples and plums, though that was certainly present. Not even the fresh-picked smell of strawberries and really good tomatoes, though I picked that up too. But it was teamed with lush smells, dipping mango and jewelled pomegranate and-
I caught that thought as it flashed past. Jewelled pomegranate was a really stupid for a girl to accept from (possibly mythological) strangers. The thought took me to Hades and Persephone, then Orpheus and Euridyce, all those classical warnings.
Don't eat the fruit.
Don't leave the path.
Don't look back.
In the silence I started to think my footsteps were the only sound left in the world, except those warnings bouncing around my mind. I couldn't hear gulls, or the wind, or the sea, so it almost came as a relief to hear a knocker's ticktock voice, just by my left hand.
"Little girl. Little girl, come leave your lantern. I have fruit dripping juice, and cakes seeping honey. How since you ate, little girl?"
My stomach answered that with a complaining growl, and I scowled. I had a couple of cereal bars stashed in my handbag, but I didn't want to eat anything in front of the- well, in front of the fairies. And I didn't want to say anything stupid in front of them either, especially anything they could construe as a deal. I had chewing gum, but all that juicy mintiness would probably make me hungrier. Looking down, I scooped up a smooth, round stone from the middle of the road, brushed it on my

jumper a bit, then popped it on top of my tongue.

I was pretty sure of two things. One, that this path was longer than it should be, by a good half mile or so. Two, despite this I was unquestionably on the right path, if the fruit-seller was any indication.

There was something glinting up ahead.

Just off the path, to the right this time, was a parrot cage, but it was filled with a single magpie, glaring balefully at me. I was less than thrilled at the omen, but walked past it, careful to keep my steps in the middle of the road. This time, I was less surprised to hear the clipped voice behind me.

"Little girl, little girl, come leave your lantern. I have here a magpie to teach you the languages of all men who ever lived. Aren't you curious, little girl?"

Yes, yes I was curious, I knew that if I turned down learning every language ever I'd wake up, maybe years from now, regretting that I'd let the opportunity fall behind me. But there was a stone in my mouth, there was a stone in my mouth and I couldn't speak.

Bitterly hating whoever offered me what I couldn't have, I kept walking, even when it started to hurt, even when I stumbled on a bit of loose gravel, even when the cold seeped into my bones, even when the drizzle started. For a while I was a drifting thing, a body dragged along on the arrowhead of my willpower. Or bloody-mindedness, but I suppose you can always swap one for another.

I could have hugged the chimney when it came into view, but I was still half-tranced with the effort of getting there.

"Sweet lady, sweet lady, come leave your lantern. Let me weave you a groom out of sea-cliff grass. Aren't you lonely, sweet lady?"

I could see the little sod this time. He sat in front of the chimney, partially blocking a hole that would be about perfect for lowering the lantern into. He was a bit bigger than Salve, his bones more pronounced at the joints, but thin nimble fingers twisted blades of grass into intricate knots.

I really hoped I wouldn't have to run at him. I jerked my thumb over my shoulder and tried to look fierce. In doing so, I swung the lantern towards him, and that, more than my expression, made him skitter away. I could still hear him though, perhaps a metre behind me.

"And what if there's nobody there, sweet lady? Will you play with us then?"

Getting impatient, I slid the coil of rope off my shoulder, and tied one end to the top handle of the lantern. I don't know a thing about knots, so I simply twisted and tightened the end- and next time, I resolved, I'd buy proper camping rope, rather than cheap wash-line rope- until I judged the handle secure.

I lay flat as I approached the hole into the mine. I was pretty sure all those alluring voices didn't have my best interests at heart, and it's pretty much impossible to trip or tip someone lying down.

I started humming round the stone in my mouth, any little songs I could think of, to try and block out the question. The sound was obviously thick and gloopy, as though I was trying to sing underwater. Still, the slightly unfamiliar noise helped distract me as I lowered the lantern down into the depths. I watched the spark of light fall further and further away, and felt my spine prickle. It's that prickle as old as mammal, the one that tells you you're in the dark and there's a predator right behind you.

The humming was whimpering now, no question about it. I should have asked the boys to do this, I decided. Salve would have taken no nonsense from his brothers, and Clem would have glided past with supreme indifference.

Count of ten, I told myself. If after a count of ten there was no response to the lantern, then I was leaving rope and lantern here and running for it. My knees ached a bit at the thought of it, but I ignored them, and counted one.

Two.

Three.

Four- wait. Something had changed in the tension of the rope. I held my breath, but nothing else was forthcoming. Perhaps I'd just hit the bottom.

Five.

Six.

Seven. There! I definite twitch on the line, Then two more, that somehow managed to transmit a slight impatience.

I took the hint, and started hauling the rope up. At that awkward angle, my arms and shoulders pistoned to not much effect, but eventually all the rope was once more lying in a coil.

Two things had been tied to the end of the rope, far more neatly than my own shoddy knotting.

The first was a small canvas bag, probably only the size of my fish. Cautiously, I pointed the mouth of the bag away from me, and loosened the drawstrings. When nothing terrible happened, I glanced into the bag, and was rewarded with the sight of pale, elegant bones jumbled together, as well as two cylinders I didn't recognise. Nearly sagging with relief, I shoved the bag slightly inelegantly into my cleavage. Nobody was pickpocketing me of anything vital on the way back to the car.

The other item gave me pause. I'd never fired a gun in real life, but there was something odd and blocky about this one- ah, it fired flares. It had one flare loaded into it, as I discovered when I sat up and examined it. Looking at the single shot, I realised that the two mystery cylinders in with the bones were also flares.

Three flares. Better and better.

I coiled the rope, slung it over my shoulder, and silently apologised to my knees. The stone was still in place, and I was a little surprised at how used to it I'd become. Luckily, it was too small to cause any drooling or anything else- though at this point, I was perfectly happy to sacrifice my dignity in return for not being kidnapped by vengeful kobolds.

I pointed the flare pistol in about the right direction. I suspected accuracy wasn't among it's principal virtues, but it would do as both short-term illumination, and disincentive for anything to mess with me.

I fired it, and nearly cracked my wrist with a recoil that wasn't terribly severe, but was a damn sight more than I'd expected. Still, the path back to the car lit up, and I was sure I heard little screeches of things not used to sudden bright light. I didn't waste time, running down the gravel road as fast as my increasingly protesting joints would let me.

Darkness settled round me again, and I slowed, checked, always checking that I hadn't left the road, and also careful not to look behind me. It was like a nightmare- my hindbrain was still telling me the predator was right behind me, but I was hazily convinced that if I didn't look behind and see it, I'd be all right.

There was a sound behind me. The sound of metal knocking on stone. I couldn't judge how close it was, I couldn't see, and I was getting confused. Only one thing for it, to my mind. I fished out a flare, walking steadily as I loaded up the gun slightly clumsily. Then I pointed it in front of me, and fired.

No doubt about it, those were screeches of pain and outrage. I was clearly pissing someone off, I just hoped I was putting them off at the same time. More importantly at that moment though, I'd spotted the shiny finish of the hire car's paint job, and that was enough to get me running again, running down the true path.

Keys! Where in the name of wisdom had I put my keys? I wasted seconds slowing to pat my jeans pockets, before realising I'd gone and left them in the ignition. Ah well, I reasoned, we were miles away from the nearest human, and the chances of the fairies wanting to get inside what was effectively a cage of iron? Not high.

Which meant, logically, that they'd have to grab me in the moment before I got into the car.

Even before I finished the conscious thought, my hands started grabbing for the last flare. I was going to have to time this precisely. I uncoiled about two metres of the rope, and hefted it loosely in my right hand. In my left hand I held the flare gun. Poor weapons, but I was getting in that car if it killed me.

I should have been more surprised when I approached the car, and saw that there was a grinning figure, looking like a grey, hunched version of Salve, lounging against the driver's side door. The resemblance to Salve might have slowed me down if I hadn't been so furious. I waxed as wrathful as I could around the stone, and flicked out the end of the rope like a whip. It caught the knocker across the cheek, and he squealed. I whipped it back at him, and this time he caught it with a grin.

Good boy, I thought with a sort of savage cheer, and used his own grip to yank him away from the door, and onto the road.

He froze, as though paralysed, while I shook off the rest of the rope, and lunged for the door. Instead of opening it, I turned to face my pursuers at last, and fired a flare straight up.

There was nobody visible, but the screams were unquestionably louder. I lost no time diving into the car and switching on both the internal light and the headlights on full beam.

The adrenaline backwash made me hands shake, and made me gulp awkwardly around the stone. I removed it gratefully, and tossed it lightly onto the passenger seat while I clicked the seatbelt home and fired the engine gratefully.

I reversed as far as I dared, keeping my headlights on the scene, until I could finally turn and run home.

I didn't make it home, mind. In fact I made it as far as the services before exhaustion, fear, and low blood sugar laid me low and left me sobbing in the services car park for twenty minutes. Eventually I managed to get a hold on myself, if only because shaking like a jelly at an earthquake's birthday party (he's invited all his little seismic friends, except the one at the back of his class who always eats the lava) reminded me where the bones were.

Slightly embarrassed, I fished them out and looked at them. There had to be at least a finger there, and several smaller bones, and the thought made me smile. We were getting closer, no question. Soon Clem wouldn't have to put up with a crystal prosthetic any more, he could have his real hand back. And as I spent a couple of minutes laying out the bones on the dashboard to see if they fit together, I realised that I felt better for having something of Clem's around me.

"That's officially pathetic," I decided, and went to see if I could grab an early breakfast.

Chapter Nine

At quarter to ten on Sunday morning, I was up, dressed, and already poking the bone compass. Salve watched me with interest.
"Like calls to like?" He waved at the compass, pulling a face at it, and the thumb wobbled slightly.
"I just hope this one's going to be a bit less hassle," I sighed. "One more fairy deal and I was about ready to go spare."
"Sorry," mumbled Salve. I cast a glance at him. One week installed in my spare room, and already he was starting to lose the stilted speech patterns. Truthfully, I wasn't sure if rooming with a not-really-fallen was such a great idea, but Salve could have been worse, no question about it. He waved cheerfully at me, and I realised I'd been scrutinising him a little more closely than was polite.
"Clem's here," Salve reported, and five seconds later a knock issued from the front door. This time, Clem had swapped the jacket for a waistcoat that could, when the light hit it right, be mistaken for a very pale blue. Thin mother-of-pearl buttons kept it fastened.
Why was I noticing this nonsense?
"It's the weekend once again." His voice was impassive, but there was a slight juddering tension in his shoulders. "Have you any ideas where to go next?"
I'd already had the maps out. I worked on the theory that the bone compass might be more effective if Clem wasn't anywhere near. I wondered vaguely where Clem went when he wasn't with me, whether he just sort of basked on a cloud somewhere or whether he ran lots of other little side-events. Perhaps there were half a dozen women like me, human agents

unaware of one another. The thought gave me a hot little anger-prickle, and I put it to one side.

"The compass keeps pointing to this symbol on the map." I carefully popped a pin in a blue square with a leafy white twig in it.

"An oaken grove?" asked Salve.

"Nope, National Trust property." I beamed at the two angels. "Time to dig up my membership card."

Isham house was a nice day out, and considering how close it was from my town, I quietly kicked myself that I didn't visit more often. It certainly made a pleasant change from the psychic museum, since I could expect a lot fewer elementals, and a lot more diligently cared-for antiquities. I was entirely happy with this idea.

I wasn't keen on the idea of guided tours, they always go at the wrong pace for me, but Clem was quietly insistent. We didn't have one guide for the whole tour, rather a series of women in blue cardigans showed up from one room to the next, relaying us to the next waiting cardigan. At first I felt a bit disoriented, but I realised that having one guide to a room meant that each guide was an absolute expert within their particular domain, even down to knowing when the fireplace was last restored, or where the third salt cellar along came from.

Clem's hand was tight on my arm. "This place was holy once, but hasn't been for a while."

"You being immortal and all, how long is a while to you, exactly?"

Clem took step nearer the front, and I noticed how people instinctively made room for him. "Excuse, me, madam? What was this house before it was a noble's estate?"

The guide smiled at the reasonably intelligent question. "Up until the 1500s, this was a monastery. Henry the Eighth dissolved it, as he did all monasteries, and gave it to a favourite at court, Sir Elgar Isham."

I felt Clem flinch next to me. So that was who took his hand, and now I thought of it, Nana Sophie had mentioned the name when translating his notes.

The guide hadn't noticed Clem's discomfort, though a collective shudder ran through the rest of the tourist party, even if none of them could have said why. Instead, she continued blithely, clearly glad to be spared the script for another moment or two. "Generally speaking, most of the treasures were stripped out of the dissolved Catholic monasteries, though in this case the Isham family asked specifically to keep the lead ceiling. Soon you'll be taken to the old chapel, where the disastrous fire of 1816 stripped away several layers of ceiling, to reveal some of the lead roof."

I tapped the head of my walking stick nervously, a habit I've been trying to suppress since I was about twenty. Lifted holy high, indeed. "They kept the chapel?"

"It's not really my room," said the guide cheerfully. "But you'll be shown extensively round it later in the tour."

Clem and I composed ourselves in patience. I admired paintings and early wallpaper, tried not to mentally price up marbles fetched back from some Victorian boy's Grand Tour, or the tin Christmas toys given to a 1930's descendant. A couple of the vases were poor reproductions, but after a certain amount of internal wrestling I decided not to draw any further attention to myself.

Through a cool stone corridor yet another guide shepherded us, and for a few steps I was quite happy to be amused by the way my walking stick tapped on the flagstones. Clem wasn't soundless, exactly, but I noticed everyone else's footsteps were much louder, as though he was only appearing to touch the earth for the sake of appearances.

He squeezed my arm briefly again, and yet another guide- male, for a change- stood up from the chair he'd been perched on attentively "Hello everyone," he murmured, sounding for all the world like a chaplain come to take services, "welcome to the chapel."

I'd half-expected something spacious smelling of incense and opulently decorated in a Catholic style. Or, due to the long-ago fire, some lingering smell of holy smoke.

In fact, I was completely wrong. The layers of the ceiling, all the restoration and alteration over the centuries, were neatly exposed in a cross-section near a high beam of the roof. We all went "ooh" in a polite fashion. It was the only interesting feature, the rest of the chapel being furnished in a particularly grey and austere fashion.

The guide droned on about his subject without any noticeable passion. "Charles the First believed in beauty and obedience. He married a Catholic, and this convinced the public that he was trying to lead the country away from Protestantism. Eventually when Puritans swept through the country under Cromwell, beheading Charles the king as they went, this chapel was emptied of all statues, relics and idols."

I exchanged glances with Clem. Relics were traditionally the bones and bits of saints, weren't they? It wouldn't be too much of a stretch to suppose there was reverence for the bones of an angel. And if your chapel was getting sacked on a semi-regular basis, then it made sense to stash it in the lead in the roof. Even if it was found, I guessed you could derive some satisfaction from the thought that the thief would be tempting a dose of lead poisoning, but in those days I wasn't convinced they understood the danger.

"I've seen lead roofs put in before," murmured Clem. "The men who fitted such things couldn't write their own names, so they drew round the soles of their shoes, sometimes put the date."

I looked around discreetly but there was no sign of any cameras. "We need to stay in the chapel. Any ideas?"

"Just the one. Take two steps to your left."

Those two steps took me to a small alcove that had presumably once contained the image of a saint or apostle. Clem stood behind me, then with a swishing sound that I probably imagined, brought his wings around me.

I was surrounded all of a sudden, in a thick, soft, soundless duvet of white down. Curiously, there was no sign of the rest of Clem, but there was an intangible presence of him, like hearing a familiar voice in the next room. The sense memory of touching him outside Bluebell retirement village came back to me, and I closed my eyes for a long breath, savouring what threatened to drown me.

Clem's wings then parted, and I had to suppress an audible sound of disappointment. We'd no doubt have to catch up to the rest of the tour party, so I stepped cautiously out into the chapel.

There was nobody there. The guides were gone, the lights were out, except for a few dim spot of illumination clumsily taped to the cordoned-off areas.

I blinked, and looked around. "Where is everyone? And where's your jacket, for that matter?"

"They closed the house to visitors four hours ago. Even the security guard has retreated to the coffee machine."

I stared at him. "Four hours? What? I was in there a minute, if that."

"I thought you might get bored waiting," Clem shrugged, in that way of his that showed that his shoulder muscles slipped under his tailoring in a distinctly inhuman manner.

I simmered with annoyance. "You shut my brain down for over four hours." I did some very quick maths. "Actually, more like seven. Don't you ever do that again. I really, really mean it." Another thought occurred to me. "And so that's how you got me back to my house with the elementals."

"I didn't mean to disturb you. I apologise, Helen."

"Hmph." I sat on a chair probably meant for a guide. I wasn't feeling it, but I'd been standing with my knees for seven hours. If I suffered for it later, I was about ready to see if I could render my winged wonder into something altogether more oven-ready.

Clem drifted gently up from the floor until his eyes were level with the cross-section of lead. "Where should I start?"

My eyes drifted up across the plasterwork. "There's a bit of a ceiling rose over the altar. Makes sense, the altar is a natural focal point of any chapel, plus it's built into the structure. Even the most zealous vandal wouldn't, and probably couldn't, budge the altar. Landmark like that would make the reliquary simple to find."

Thoughtfully, Clem probed the ceiling rose. Calling it a rose was probably being kind, it was more of a crudely-shaped bobble in the plaster. Presumably it had once had more definition, but successive layers of player and paint had blurred the fine detailing.

Clem was in no mood for a spot of architectural appreciation. "I dislike rummaging through old chapels. I...can't help thinking that the masons, plasterers, sculptors, painter, woodworkers, all of them didn't mean for their, their *devotion*, to be ripped apart by amateur treasure seekers."

I tested my joints gingerly. Everything seemed to be holding up all right thus far. "Sounds like I'm missing some subtext."

Clem backed off a little, looking back into the cross section. The lead was more or less flush with the layers below it- I could swear among the brick and the wood I saw honest-to-goodness wattle and daub- yet Clem removed his gloves and slid his crystalline hand easily between the non-existent gap.

"Like calls to like," he muttered. "You may have a point about subtext. It's nearly impossible for an angel to create things, you see. We are made to preserve. And obey. And sing in adoration."

"Do you get to make up the songs, at least?" Watching Clem's hand made my stomach creep from the wrongness of it, so I watched his absorbed expression.

"Standard liturgy, I'm afraid. Ah, here we are."

He removed a slim canister, looking for all the world like a dull, light grey cigar case. I wasn't too keen on touching it, so I got yet another handful of tissues, and caught it as Clem half-passed, half threw it at me.

I nearly fumbled the catch. "Damn, that's heavy."

"The cannister is lead as well. Perhaps they didn't want the holiness leaking out? Or, more likely, a lead object is easiest to hide amongst lead. And don't swear in church, please, Helen."

I quirked a little smile at his tone. "There's worse been done in here."

"That's no excuse to succumb," Clem snapped, turned and made to leave. I grabbed his shirt sleeve.

"Woah, there, how do you plan to leave the building?"

"Would you think less of me if I said 'in flames'? Sir Elgar bought this with the severed remains of my hand. I want to smite this place into the dust and then salt the earth. Knowing that he and his family prospered-" Clem took a deep, albeit biologically meaningless breath. "Nonetheless. Ego sum clementia. I am mercy."

Ignoring his sudden spark of temper- and who wouldn't be annoyed, in Clem's place?- I rifled through my handbag again. I had a hazy idea I'd picked up- yes, an extra £1.50 on entry bought a small guide book. Well, more of a leaflet, really, but I seldom minded. I rather liked the colourful and glossy paper; sometimes in the throes of shop-bound boredom I admired the tiny photos of perfectly preserved dining rooms.

This particular guide leaflet, however, I'd picked up for the sake of the crude fold-out map on the inside flaps. Sadly for all thieves- and it suddenly occurred to me that this was what the little lead canister made me- there was no mention of where the cameras were. Having said that, I had a better idea.

"Clem, look at this. The exits will be alarmed by now- resist the obvious joke, okay? But we don't have to leave the house. We stash ourselves somewhere discreet, further past the tour than we've already been. Then, tomorrow morning, we join an early tour. The guides in the relay will assume that we arrived with the rest of the tour. And I'd be very surprised if they notice anything missing, much less think to search visitors."

"A good idea in principle," decided Clem. "But the guard patrols most areas of the building, and the television cameras cover the exhibition rooms."

I froze over the map. "But...the chapel is an exhibition room! We're probably being recorded right now."

Clem smiled, slightly smugly. "Then I trust they enjoy a close view of my jacket."

I looked up briefly. Clem's jacket appeared to be hanging in mid air about six inches above the solid wooden door, but on seeing the (slightly unsteady) wiring disappear under the collar I realised that he'd simply hooked the thick garment over a small camera. The wash of relief as I looked back down gave the map in my hand a new focus.

"There's one place the guard won't go," I smiled, looking at the twinned symbols just down the corridor from our current location.

Clem ruffled his wings, a little uncomfortable around his hastily-recovered jacket. "The Ladies', no less. Yes, a male guard would be uncomfortable here. Truthfully, so am I."
I tucked myself as comfortable as possible into the far cubicle. "Don't you have girl angels?"
"*Those who believe not in angels name them female names* ," said Clem. It sounded as though he was quoting something, and a moment later I realised it was the Qu'ran.
"Though there is Chokkma, of course." Clem continued. "The exception to quite a lot of rules. The one female, the one angel who didn't fight, and so on." He considered a moment. "Possibly just as well. Like human warriors, we would have been...unsettled by the presence of a female in the front lines."
Much as I was enjoying the history lesson, I shushed Clem quickly as the flicker of torchlight in the corridor outside warned me of the security patrol.
I slide my cubicle door shut, not all the way to locking it, but just enough to hide me. As I suspected, the guard made a cursory sweep of the room, decades of social training telling him he couldn't come further into the room.
"I'm going to get sod all sleep like this," I grumbled.
I heard Clem shift slightly. "Once more, we're trapped in an enclosed space in the dark. Glory be."
"Sarcasm's not very angelic, you know." I smiled at the darkness. "You could always borrow a torch off the guard."
"It's all very well for you. You could simply enfold yourself in my wings, and the night would be a moment."
"No. I couldn't."

I'm sure Clem snorted, but he didn't say anything further.

I woke up on a thin carpet I didn't recognise, my back and leg cramped with cold and awkward positioning.
The front of me, in contrast, was covered with soft warmth, or perhaps warm softness, both sensations arrived equally in my brain. I batted at it faintly- then realised that what I'd sleepily taken for a duvet was in fact Clem's left wing.
"Whu?" I heard myself mumble. "Wha?"
From behind me, Clem coughed. "The cold made you shiver in your sleep. I didn't think you'd appreciate hypothermia."
I batted the wing a away, a little embarrassed. "Ah, well, thank you."
"The first tour has already begun. Judging by how fast we progressed yesterday, we need to enact your plan in about ten minutes."
I hauled myself up, grumbling. I was aware that even if we got away with this, last night I'd parked the car about half a mile away under a shady tree. I figured that if the house had CCTV anywhere, it would be in the car park, so rather than leave a car there overnight, and give people ample time to read the plates, I'd found a country lane. The obvious downside of this being that once we made our glorious getaway, we still had a ten minute walk.
Clem gave me a good-luck smile, tugged my blouse down at the back for me, and vanished from the Ladies'. I counted to fifty, and was rewarded with the sound of human voices. Quickly, I slipped out to the back of the party. Clem was already there, tucked away at the side and talking genially to a middle-aged woman in pearls.
We completed the tour at last, but even if I hadn't been too ashamed to speak, nerves dried my throat very effectively. At

one point I thought I was going to have a coughing fit, and the horror of the notion made me freeze. The fit passed in silence.

My separation from Clem continued as we walked through different exits, Clem ten steps behind me. Whereas I buried my face in the leaflet as though I'd found something fascinating to consider, Clem strolled breezily across the gravel, tipping his hat (and where did the hat come from?) at the guard in the booth by the gate.

I reached the car with no challenge, no "hey you!" from anyone behind me. Give or take some attention by the local bird population, the hire car was mercifully intact. Tired, I slumped into the sear, and waited for my nerves to unwind. "Clem, can you drive?"

Clem shook his head regretfully. "I have trouble keeping up with new technology. You'll be all right to drive, though. Take it steady, lots of little rests." He produced the small seamless canister, and peered at the expensively hand-hammered exterior. "Nice to know I'm treasured, at any rate. How do I open it?"

"I'd just pull one end off," I carefully checked my speed limit. "Lead's a soft metal, right?"

I heard something rattle, and Clem's hiss of triumph.

"How many fingers?" Most of my attention was focused on the road signs. The shop was closer than my flat, and it needed opening anyway.

"Not full fingers," he reported, "but I have a bundle of phalanges. And three metacarpals, I think."

I grimaced. "You'd think people would just buy the one finger and be done with it."

We rolled up to the shop, me noting with anxiety that it was already half nine. Would there be a queue of raging customers? I flinched at the prospect.

The door was unlocked. I used a word that made Clem flinch. Stepping forward nervously, I considered whether my insurance premiums were up to date. I reckoned they were all right, especially since I took possession of a rather fetching French fencing foil. I was sold by the sword by a boarding school, of all things, who'd been given it as a stage prop, but it was far too sharp for little hands. Hell, it was too sharp for me; I kept it in a cardboard poster tube.

The lights were on, and nothing was broken. I took another step- and Salve threw himself at me, and hugged me as though I was a long-lost love.

"Good morning! I hope you're having a lovely day, please let me make it bet- oh, hello, Helen."

I spluttered, stuck between being amused and annoyed. "Well, full marks for customer service! How did you manage all this?"

"Clem helped." Salve looked up at me like a proud child showing off his macaroni drawing.

"Clem..?" I turned and smiled sweetly at him. He recoiled slightly.

"I'll leave you be for a week."

"Good idea."

Apocrypha

More mornings passed. And evenings too, when the heat fell away from the earth, and the sky turned gold and pink and orange. Moths rose on silent wings, and butterflies took their rest after a day's soft fluttering.
Chokkma loved the garden best of all then. Smiling, she furled her wings away and stepped into the river. At first, it was enough to admire the fish, little silver flashes that came to nibble hopefully on her fingers. But as darkness grew, it became enough to lie back, float on the water- and how very different that felt to floating on the air!- and watch the stars come out.
"Lilith," growled a voice above her. "What do you do, remaining in the garden?"
With a frown, Chokkma pushed herself into the air, revealing her wings. "I'm not Lilith, Uriel. See the wings? I'm Chokkma, and I can go where I please."
Uriel was not to be moved. "You have wings. She has wings. And you both wear the same face."
Still dripping clear riverwater, Chokkma beat her wings once, and started gliding towards him. "You woke in the place of silk and silver a moment after I did, and looked upon me." They were nearly close enough to touch. "You waited a while, then told me that you liked my shape, and that you thought that perhaps there was a way our bodies could fit together."
Nearly mesmerised, Uriel's wings flared out behind him. "Yes. I did that."
"So we pressed our bodies together," continued Chokkma in an inexorable softness, "and we fit together as did the river the bank, moving and gliding against each other."

"It is you." Uriel threw one arm around her waist and pulled her close, at the same moment as Chokkma flung her arms around his neck and threw herself at him.
After a complicated few moments, Chokkma smiled against Uriel's mouth. "Now, tell me about Lilith."
"She...mmm...she would not lie beneath Adam when they coupled. She would...as you're doing, in fact."
There was a soft chuckle. "Is there anything wrong with this?"
"No...but Adam, all must bow before him, even us. She would not, she claimed equality. Please...again..."
Chokkma gave this some slightly distracted thought. "Did she quit the garden herself, or was she expelled?"
"We, oh, we found herself, riding on the back of Michael's creature, intoxicated by her own strength and- and lust. She threw garlic at us, and...uh...walked out the... gate." Uriel's breath left him in a rush, and he lay back against the grass.
"Could have been worse," laughed a very cheerful Chokkma, "she could have been riding Sam's creature. Good for Lilith, leaving on her own legs. It must be a very difficult thing to do."
Uriel sat up, his face suddenly full of sadness. "It wasn't only her who was stained by the punishment, though. Look in the river, Chokkma."
Suddenly gripped by fear, realising herself to be, after all, the most sinful angel ever, Chokkma approached the shining water. Where once her wings had been stainless white, and round as the moon, now her wings were both white and brown, the arches pointed.
"I have owl wings?" Chokkma examined them. "When did that happen?"
"A few moments ago." Uriel was suddenly very interested in the grass he'd crushed. "When you- when you were distracted."
Chokkma flapped them experimentally. "I can still fly. And I

look different to the other angels anyway. No, it doesn't bother me."

"I'm glad," said Uriel sincerely. But still, he resolved that someone else should probably tell Chokkma about Eve.

Chapter Ten

Salve patted his pockets hopefully. In the left one, he had a mobile phone, a sealed letter from me, and the address of Birch and Poet. In his right pocket, he had a quantity of cash, and a rail ticket that he currently prized as the price of passage. Apart from that, there was little between Salve and the world apart from a pair of shorts and a muddy brown shirt.

My description of Birch and Poet's house was enough that Salve didn't have any trouble finding the right place. There were new additions, too, thick black spikes topping the fencing.

"It's for the local kids," explained a voice behind Salve. "They get bored, start climbing our walls and stuff."

Metaphorical heart still hammering, Salve turned to see a woman who fitted the description of Birch perfectly. Salve gave her what he really hoped was a winning smile. Judging by the thinning of her lips, the smile wasn't even a runner up.

"Who are you, then?" She demanded.

"I'm Salve." Salve wasn't sure if he was supposed to shake her hand, kiss it, or maybe salute? He flapped his hand at her in a kind of compromise.

Birch nodded to herself. "Okay, that's my fault for asking the wrong questions. *What* are you?"

Salve was slightly flustered. "If I said I'm a knocker, there might be really rude jokes. Or ones about doors,which are just as annoying, So I have a letter."

Birch narrowed her eyes. "You open it up, thanks."

"Want me to read it out?" Salve had a little trouble with the envelope, and then squinted at my handwriting.

"Dear Birch and Poet,
The person holding this letter is Salve, he's a knocker from Cornwall, remember I was dealing with them? He's reasonably harmless, he's just going to ask you some questions about iron.
Yes, the scavenger hunt is still weird.
Thanks,
Helen."

"Ah. You're from the Scavenger." Birch opened the gate, and that was when Salve realised that Poet had been quietly listening from the door of the garage.
"We're gonna need more tea." Poet sighed.

"I have obviously been missing a hundred- no, a thousand, gorgeous taste moments." Salve eyed the bottom of his teacup. "Though that's mostly because Helen won't let me into all her condiments and rummage round."
"Have you at least bought her a drink first?" Poet poured a refill of green tea. "No, never mind. What do you need to know about iron?"
"Everything." Salve waved a hand. "I mean, I know iron is male, I think that's because it's got the same alchemical symbol for the male and for Mars, I know it lives in your blood and in the liver, and since blood is one of the four humours it's associated with moist warmth,and-"
"Science has moved on a bit since then," interrupted Poet as patiently as possible. "Is there a specific bit of iron you're interested in? It's only the sixth most abundant element in the universe, but we'd be grateful for a little narrowing down."

Salve's eyes lit up- no really, he was down in that dark mine so long they went luminous, like a glow-in-the-dark sticker, when he was excited. "Actually, yes! I want the knight that learned to sing. That's what the prophecy says."
"Oh, bollocks," groaned Poet. "There's an actual *prophecy*."
"And what's worse," added Birch, wearing much the same expression, "Is that I think we know the knight. Do you mind a little rust?"

"No, it's all right," said Salve, "The blanket is comfy."
Birch and Poet had a van, but it only had two seats in it. So for the twenty minute trip, Salve had opted to perch on a blanket on the back. The blanket was a little thread worn, and still had the faint smell of elderly spaniel, but Salve was happy to loll on it and watch the scenery shrink away from the rear-view windows.
Birch and Poet rode in silence, Poet driving, but Salve didn't particularly think it rude. Someone would have to seriously crick their neck to have a conversation with him, even assuming sound would carry from the front of the van to the back.
Twenty minutes later, the scenery began to slow, before the van dawdled to a halt. Salve scrabbled upright just as Birch opened the door.
"We're here," she said cheerfully. "You might want to watch where you're stepping."
'Here' was an old scrap metal yard. Salve took an experimental breath, and got a lungful of iron oxide.
"Smells like an irony place. Is it really old?"
"Not really," explained Poet. "It's from the Second World War. The Government took down all the wrought iron railings they could find, told everyone they were being made for munitions

and such. It was part of the war effort, encouraged everyone to conserve their metals. But it was mostly propaganda, the railings were often dumped out the way. Now we reforge a lot of this stuff, recycle and reclaim anything we can."

"That not to say there's not a guard," continued Birch. "Come and see."

The guard was silent and still, his feet tangled in place by ivy and quite a healthy oak sapling. At first glance, Salve thought it was a suit of armour, then he saw that the chest was a beaten-down car bonnet, the eyes were old electric bulbs. The limbs were reshaped bumpers and even the raised, half-clenched fist had it's fingers made of chainsaw parts.

A stray breeze caught Birch's hair, and the slumping ivy, but most of all it made an echo chamber of the misshapen chest and whistled out in a lonely sound.

Salve felt his teeth prickle, and knocked his knuckles gently on a nearby piece of steel. The tiny concussions of his power bounced back, and spoke of a tiny, nearly atrophied magic.

Salve circled it warily. "Why is this golem here?"

"It looks like scrap," pointed out Poet. "If you didn't know it was animate, why not send it to the scrapyard? Then it realises it's moved, doesn't know any better, so starts guarding the scrap yard."

Birch compassionately tapped one rusting foot. "Only it doesn't know what it's supposed to guard against, so it gets into positions and waits for further instructions that never come. Poor bugger."

The golem creaked deliberately, and all three of them fell back. This time though, there were words behind the whistling voice.

"Born in armour, laid on gold,
Breath so roasting, blood so cold."

"Dragon," chorused Poet and Salve together, and then blinked at each other.

Birch frowned. "Why is it giving us a riddle?"

"Holly-conquered, summer king,
Acorn-scioned, pillar sings."

"Um, the summer King is the lord of Oak," began Birch.

"And the wind through the branches probably sounds like singing to this knight," mused Poet.

"An oak-tree then," decided Salve.

"Silver-tongued, double speech,
Born to aid a hero's reach."

"A sword, maybe?" Poet frowned. "Could be several things."

"Look at the angles of his hand." Salve stepped closer. "That's not how you hold a sword, you'd lose an eye. It's how you'd hold a lance."

"Or a spear," murmured Birch.

The knight held it's peace.

"A dragon, an oak tree, and a spear." Poet shook his head. "Nope, not seeing a connection."

Birch counted points on her fingers. "Add in a princess and a horse and you've pretty much got a knight's wish list. I mean, not a real knight, you'd need more beer and wenches, but the sort of fairytale this golem was based on."

Salve wasn't listening. "I've forgotten trees, but isn't that a baby oak?"

Birch and Poet both turned to the sapling.

"Funny thing," said Poet evenly. "That old exhaust in the undergrowth there, just under the sapling?"

"...Would be about the size of a lance." Birch finished. "The golem wants arming, and because it's shaped like a knight, it wants to save the lady from a monster."

"We've got a lady!" Salve beamed at Birch, and ignored Poet's coughing fit. "And Poet could be the squire, handing over the weapon. And I'd make a great monster."

The humans' faces were eloquent in their scepticism.

Ta-da!" Salve sang brightly, and revealed his wings.

Birch and Poet looked at him dubiously, so he flapped his stubby bat wings hopefully.

Poet put his head to one side. "Can you get any lift on these things, or are they more like rudders?"

"Never mind, Salve," said Birch kindly. "Maybe we can just cuddle."

Salve felt his face fall. "All right, all right. Maybe I should have had more keratin in my diet, and less damnation, but they're the only wings we've got, and I don't think Sir Scrapyard there ever saw a real dragon."

Birch tried to look contrite. "I'm sorry, there. Poet, go stand by the lance. Salve, menace me."

Salve stood on tiptoes, spread his wings and went "grr" in what was probably a lot being menaced by baby deer. Baby deer being ridden by kittens.

Nonetheless, Birch did her bit, getting into the knight's line of sight, then cowering theatrically. "Oh, no!" she enunciated. "Save me, save me!"

"Oh, for..." Poet rolled his eyes. "We'll be tying you to the railway tracks next."

"Promises promises," whispered Birch.

"Trying...not..to...laugh!" Salve hissed.

It was enough to fool the golem. With a rage of stressed metal, the knight stepped from his plinth, and roared to find his hand empty.

"It's here, Sir Knight!" Poet passed him the lance, and Salve could have hugged him to see that Poet had covered that terrifying tip with the kind of sponge-foam more usually found inside car seats.

The knight didn't care, nor did he then stab with the spear, instead he raised it above his head and brought it down like a massive club.
"Roll!" Birch screamed.
Salve rolled- but still had his wings out. He heard the sharp snapping sound as the weapon connected, heard a series of other crashes- and then the pain arrived.
"Poet, it's his wing." Now in genuine crisis, Birch was loud but unhurried. "I heard it break from here. You help Salve, I'll sort out the knight."
Poet was instantly next to the stricken Salve. "Salve, can you hear me?"
"Yes-yes." Salve's teeth were chattering. "Sha...king. Sh-shock?"
"Yes, you're going into shock, but I need you to stay with me for a little bit, all right? I'm going to left the spear off, see what the damage is, okay?"
"Okay." Salve considered, not bursting into tears exactly, but certainly having a little pained snivel in a corner somewhere.
"Lifting in three...two...one..." Poet quickly and firmly unpinned Salve from the ground. Salve lifted his heard and barked a curse that changed the prevailing weather fronts.
"You're doing well." Poet's reassurance was professional but genuine. "I'm going to check the injury now. Now, before I start, I want you to tell me how much it hurts out of ten, with ten being the worst pain you can imagine."
Salve gave this some thought. "Six."
"Okay, let me know if that number gets any higher." Poet started feeling along the wing. "There's very little bleeding, you've just got a graze. Still, it's rusty metal. Do knockers get tetanus shots?"
"We don't get tetanus at all, we can't be diseased."

"Okay, that's good." Poet could see where the break was. "Without an X-ray, I can tell you it looks like a clean break. I'm going to assume that knockers have the same bone structure as humans."

Birch was rifling through a heap of steel. "But that's a wing."

"Bat wings have a similar muscle structure to human arms and hands. Assuming no difference between bat wing and knocker wing bones, I'd say you've broken your...radius. Looks like the radius and ulna are more fused in a wing. We're going to splint it up."

"Oh, perfect." Salve looked woebegone at the prospect. "Be honest, Doc. Will I ever soar through the endless vaults of Heaven again?"

Poet held up a straight piece of metal with a speculative expression. "I don't see why not."

Salve beamed. "That's fantastic! I didn't know I could un-Fall. Still, modern medicine can do wonders these days!"

"Hate to burst your bubble," smiled Birch, "but I don't think you can get a Fall-ectomy on the NHS."

"Hmm," pondered Salve. "You think I should go private?" He grunted. "What are you bandaging that with?"

There was a vague ripping noise. "Gaffer tape. It'll hold better until we can get proper bandages, and I like this shirt too much to rip strips off it." Poet looked over Salve's good wing and mouthed to Birch, "Keep him talking."

"Hey, it's not all bad news. I mean, unless you're the knight. The impact shattered him to pieces; I think the weeds were probably all that was holding him together. I've found a bunch of chalky bones wired into various bits of him."

"Animated with angel bones." Salve nearly flapped his wings thoughtfully, before a stab of pain advised him that was a bad plan. "Is there anything you can't use them for?"

Birch gave this some fascinated thought. "I really, really hope we never have to find out."

As Salve delicately lifted out the bones, a stray breeze caught at the twisted metal, and he wondered if could hear the knight's voice as it dwindled.

"What is forged may shattered be,
To be unforged is false mercy.
Lest past to present ends up banned,
Do not reforge that sought-out..."

Chapter Eleven

Research wasn't helping me in the least. Copper was, as Clem pointed out, the metal of Venus, so looking up the alchemy of copper gave me the symbol that meant copper, or Venus, or female, or Friday, depending on context.

Besides, now I looked again at the translation, I was about worried about this business with the maids who die. I wasn't a maid, having had a moderate amount of sex (back in University- my personal life was starting to look like something I'd sell in the shop) thought I supposed I did apply in the ancient Celtic sense of never having had any children.

Grumbling, I pulled the jar towards me. Picking all the while at the now-illegible peanut butter label, I tried counting the bones we'd accumulated so far. It seemed to me we only had finger bones, and I was pretty sure there were a whole bunch of little bones at the bottom, where the hand joined the wrist. I couldn't be entirely sure what we had, in truth, since the tiny bones drifted along on currents that weren't actually there.

I wished that Salve hadn't dismantled the bone compass, not least because I wasn't sure what he'd done with the mercury. Knowing Salve, he probably just tipped it down the sink. God, I hoped not, that stuff could be absorbed through the skin. Always assuming the fumes didn't get you first.

I peered into the jar and addressed the tiny sticks of calcium. "Look lads, I'm not Clem, but if you give me any crap I'm going to pour cheap cola in there and start shaking. I need some useful Brownian motion to find the copper bones. I'd give you a coin to work with, but pennies are only copper-plated steel these days."

Particle theory probably wasn't Clem's strong point, because any attempt at true Brownian motion was swiftly abandoned in favour of the bones dropping as though puppet strings had been cut. They tried to awkwardly pile over one particular location on the map, and I had to lift the jar off the paper to see. This proved almost impossible, despite being a cheap round of glass, a thin plastic lid, and a series of finger bones no heavier than hill-chalk.

"Really cheap cola," I threatened. "We're talking shop's own brand here."

The jar lifted, and I stared down at the result.

I couldn't help noticing that a lot of people related to this quest had nicer houses than me. Though I'll admit that's not hard since I'm living in a two-bedroom flat just outside a small town.

The Čachtice Institute was no Isham House, but it must have been a decent country home at one point, before being turned into what looked like a health spa. Sure, there were women strolling along in particularly stylish nurses' uniforms, but none of the middle-aged and elderly patients looked actually ill. Most of them had the sleek, well groomed look of people tolerating an interruption to their golf afternoons.

I had no clue how I was going to get in there. Even with my frizzy hair in a plait and my best (all right, only) walking cane by my side, I wasn't built for stealth. There was pretty much only one option, and I took it by marching in through the gate, chin raised and lippy freshly applied.

The receptionist looked up and my face, down at my shoes, then he sighed and put the top back on his fountain pen. "Are you with the media?"

"Not at all." I matched my tone to his. "I'm trying to obtain some literature for my father. He's not staying in that retirement village a moment longer."

"I'm afraid this is a private institute."

Quite a large orderly was looking across at us in a reasonably unsubtle way. I held up my hands in a peaceful gesture. "Fine. Honestly, Daddy's Oxbridge societies were less trouble than this. Good day."

I turned to go- and the orderly punched me lightly on the shoulder blade. "Yes, yes, I'm...I'm leaving..."

I felt my legs go, not just my knees but my whole legs, scraping my shin in a curiously painless way on the corner of the reception desk as I fell. That wasn't a punch, was it? I'd been put under sedation enough times to know he must have been holding a syringe of something interesting.

I marshalled a lingering fluffy thought, right down into my lungs. "Run," I whispered, and felt myself exhale sharply.

"Not in that state, you're not." I couldn't see the receptionist, but his voice told me he was smiling.

I wasn't talking to you, I thought, before the last of my mind sank into clouds.

Chapter Twelve

Clemael wasn't at all surprised to find himself near his last sighting of Solomon. Because it had to be, hadn't it? The old king had been noticeably absent so far, having so dramatically declared himself an enemy of the enterprise.
Clem beat his wings thoughtfully, gaining height in regular beats. "You're an ancient, cunning, empowered nephilim," he told himself. "You've set yourself against the angel of Mercy, and now you have something he really, really wants. And will have. So..."
He closed his eyes, and stretched out his hands, flesh and crystal. He didn't technically need to do that, but it reminded him of younger days, when the choices were easier and he'd never taken a wound.
There! Almost nothing, certainly nothing to be seen. But half a mile away sat a small hillock, half-invisible under a clump of trees and brambles. But under the trees was a hollow, a cold vacuum from which Clem's senses could find nothing. No worms worked the soil, according to that cold spot, no microbes bred in the tree roots, nor insects crawled, nor moss and lichens grew, where that cold spot was. The trees and brambles might just as well have grown on an iceberg.
Grinning his triumph, Clem swooped low and dug his hands into the soil. A bramble plant toppled onto him, but Clem ignored the pain, holding it away from him as best he could with his crystal hand. It hurt just as much, but quartz didn't bleed.
With the undergrowth cleared away, two parallel depressions became clear in the ground. Clem didn't know that they proved the waste ground had once been a railway line, but he knew

that two paths like that would be perfect to navigate a chariot down. Which meant the door had to be...

Ten paces yielded up a hatch set into a concrete platform.

Glad he wasn't carrying around a fragile human, Clem threw open the hatch, and jumped right in.

And was dazzled.

Clem vaguely recognised the shape of the space as a temple structure, but the exact dimensions took a while to work out, because everything, every surface, every object, every furnishing, was made of solid, gleaming silver. Clem's own grey morning suit was the closest the room had to colour.

Cautiously, Clem stepped among the pillars as though in a hall of mirrors. He had to concede admiration for the artistry involved, not to mention the maintenance- there was probably enough polishing to go round. But then, Solomon often bound djinn to his service, didn't he?

Once past the pillars, the space opened out before a dais, on top of six shallow steps. Clem wasn't surprised to see that the steps had two half-life-sized animal statues on them each. It was clear that Solomon was, if nothing else, a creature of habit. Then again, the original Throne of Solomon heavily featured lions and eagles. This one seemed to favour... Clem squinted. Foxes, badgers, otters, wyverns, moles, deer, and sundry other beasts of British wildlife posed in gleaming glory, all facing each other across the wide, flat steps.

Not bothering to breathe, Clem placed one elegantly-shod foot on the lowest step.

"Not yet," said a nearby voice. Clem turned to find himself being addressed by the fox.

"What's not-?"

"Clemael," said the otter over him, "When once you hear this, Salve will be injured-"

"What? How?"

"-And my little coz will be near death," intoned an adder. There was a tiny whistling breeze, and Clem saw a sylph resting in the adder's coils. It was slumped in a wheezy heap, as though it had just fled a long distance. "A horrific death, moreover."

This is an answering phone message, decided Clem. Solomon's probably somewhere else entirely. He looked into the deer's eyes and shuddered. That didn't mean Solomon wasn't watching.

"What's happening to Salve and Helen?" He demanded.

There was no reply.

"All right then," he mused aloud. "Salve's already been injured, I can't-yet- stop that. But I can save Helen now. And Solomon? I will return for what's mine."

For a moment, the eyes of the deer saw only pounding wings.

Chapter Thirteen

I dozed a little bit. Still groggy, I was nonetheless clear on one thing: nothing good was going to happen to me once I opened my eyes. So I decided to put off any unpleasantness for a little bit longer, and try to enjoy these last few moments of peace.
It was no good, I was lying on a cold floor, and there were a lot of people whimpering and bumping into me.
I cracked open a weary eye- and found my face was a few centimetres from a sturdy wire mesh. It folded neatly into a cube, and a second eye informed me I was lying in the bottom of a cage.
"And I've run out of suitable swearwords already," I mumbled at someone's shoes. The shoes in question were undoubtedly feminine, as were most of the shoes sharing the cage with me. And that was only if I gave the intermittent pairs of trainers the benefit of doubt. I risked sitting up, very slowly, and viewed enough shins and knees to convince me that this was an all-female holding area.
I treated myself to a little flicker of relief. At least nobody in here was going to be taking liberties. And it had to be said that apart from my cane, I still had all the clothes and accessories I'd come in with. Another flicker of relief scattered across my mind.
A scream cut through the background fright, but not the drunk screams that I'd learnt to ignore as my drunken neighbours entirely failed to negotiate the stairs up to their front door. This was a sober scream, the scream of a woman in immediate and serious trouble, and it instantly had the effect of a fistful of stimulants on my groggy senses.
Standing, fingers clutching the wire mesh for support, I saw the

girl who screamed.

She'd been dumped on some sort of conveyor belt about ten feet up, her feet shackled to a butcher's hook. The girl struggled, and with a shriek ended up hanging from the belt by her feet, swaying and red-faced.

There was a bucket. Oh God.

There was a bucket on the the floor, under the conveyor belt from which the girl now swung. I saw it was there, but I couldn't make my brain figure out what a deep, steel bucket could be used for. I knew it wasn't for cleaning, there was no mop and it was empty. I couldn't stop staring at it.

One of the acolytes walked up the girl, grunting now as she tried to find a position that didn't leave her dizzy. He grabbed her hair, forcing her head back, then raised his other hand, suddenly gripping a bowie knife, and slashed across her throat.

The blood was instant. It didn't just fall into the bucket, this was blood under pressure and already pooling in that direction, this blood hurled itself downwards as though glad to be free, in a gush of sound and colour.

We started screaming then, me included. We screamed like animals; didn't sound like human women at all. We couldn't think; we were all cramped and panicking and the panic-waves sloshed back and forth, drowning out any chance of coherent thought.

I'm not sure how long this lasted, probably less than a minute, before the sheer futility of rattling at the mesh cage calmed us down. Someone was still gabbling in a language I didn't know, though I suspected it was Polish. The rest of us settled down into muffled sobs.

I made myself look at the bucket again, I had to know what happened to it next. If I could understand what was going on, maybe I could out-think it or something. So even though it was the thing I wanted to look at least in the world, the drained corpse having been removed while we panicked and thrashed, I stared at it.

It could have been paint that sat in the bucket. I let myself believe that it was, just a little bit, just enough so I could see what happened.

The far end of the room had, so far, been screened, the kind of nondescript divider used when space doesn't allow for a workplace to have separate offices. Two female acolytes came and removed the screen, revealing steps that dropped into a flat red-brown depression from which steps led out. Then the male acolyte poured the contents of the bucket between the steps, and I saw that the red-brown panel was a still pool of human blood.

Apart from the sheer horror of it being a pool of human blood (and that was the kind of horror that froze the skin) it was the sheer annoyance that it wasn't being collected for anything useful. You couldn't get anything medical out of sloshing all the blood together like that, no scientific analysis or investigation could take place. It was there for a purpose not scientifically valid, and despite everything I'd seen and learnt, that offended my rational sensibilities.

The two female acolytes reappeared, this time at the head of a small, unsteady procession. Withered old men and women in bathrobes shuffled, bright eyed, in a rough line. A couple of the women in the other cages looked away, not wanting to see what the acolytes would do to people who looked like their grandparents.

I kept looking. These people were being treated like people, not like chicken in the slaughterhouse, and that made me think that maybe they'd get a better deal than us. The first one, an old lady bent almost double, slipped off her bathrobe, and ignoring her own nakedness, took a few trembling moments to descend the steps into the pool of blood.

The pool was deeper than I'd estimated; she was a good five foot but the blood was up to her waist, then her breasts, shoulders, chin, and then finally she was completely submerged, not even a swirl of grey hair breaking the surface.

The acolytes, old and young, watched with hungry expressions.

I'd counted to three under my breath before the surface of the blood broke for a human figure. I didn't understand at first, drugged and scared and stupid. Then I saw the pretty young woman, emerging like an obscene Venus, smile at the Horae-nurse standing with a robe.

Private institute, indeed. Getting old? Go submerge yourself in the blood of murdered women, you'll lose fifty years in three seconds. Come back as your own daughter, or even granddaughter, and all you have to do is keep paying the yearly subscription to enjoy all the benefits of immortality.

I'd seen enough. If there was any chance of getting out of here, it had to be taken now. But there was no way I was getting out without help.

"Clemael, come to me," I whispered, making it a murmuring chant I could keep up for ages if need be. "Clemael, come to me, Clemael..."

It occurred to me that most summoning were in Latin. What was the Latin for 'come to me'? Was it 'veni', something like that?

"Veni, Clemael, Clemael veni. Veni, veni, Clemael, veni, veni, Clemael, veni, veni..." I felt the chant settle into a natural rhythm, matching my breath until all the air in my lungs rolled with the words. I couldn't help feeling glad that little elemental in my lungs had taken my advice and run for it. What terrible use could the Čachtice Institute put a sylph to?

To my surprise, a woman behind me was trying to pick up the chant, then another woman to the side copied her, soon it didn't matter if the rest of the prisoners couldn't hear or pronounce the syllables properly, the suruss of frightened girls chanting for their lives, begging for help in quiet, beaten voices, filled the air.

"Veni, veni, Clemael. Veni, veni..."

As I brushed it against the mesh of the cage, my shin sharply announced that it was still grazed, and the slight shock gave me the idea to fight blood with blood. Still chanting, I collected little smears of blood on my fingertips, and clumsily daubed CLEMAEL on the concrete floor. Actually, it started out CLEMEAL, twenty-five years of the English language compelling me to put the E before the A.

"Veni, veni, Clemael. Veni, veni..."

The younger-looking acolytes had finally noticed us. The man with the bowie knife gestured to the cages. "You lot can pack it in, right now."

"Yes," said a voice just behind him, "their grasp of Latin is off-putting, isn't it?"

Clem stepped out from behind the astonished acolyte, flicking the bowie knife out of his hand with a fancy move of his sword. I'd never seen Clem armed before, the sword was slim, straight-bladed, and the metal shone with such a mirror-like finish so that even the feeble fluorescent tube that served as lighting made it look as though the sword was on fire.

"Clem!" I shrieked, trying to warn him. Informative, aren't I?

One of the newly rejuvenated rushed Clem in a blood-steeped frenzy, but with an elegant precision Clem stepped to one side. The acolyte barrelled past him, crashing into the cages. Clem made a tiny gesture, and the crashing reverberated through the cages making the door wobble and fall from their hinges.

The rest of the Institute wasn't stupid. In the face of an unstoppable swordsman and two dozen furious women, most of them fled, in various states of undress.
"Reach down, and look up," suggested Clem.
I obeyed, and my hand brushed something, about three feet off the ground. A round metal thing.
Looking down, I saw I was holding a sword-pommel.
A number of the other women had made the same discovery. Growing out of the concrete at our feet were a series of swords that had the same shape as Clem's sword, but not as shiny, and I as hefted the blade experimentally, I suspected it was a bit too light to be decent metal as well.
There was a growl from my fellow prisoners, and it came from my throat too.
"This," said Clem very quietly, as we raised our blades, "is known as the rage of angels."

I'd been all up for the carnage that followed, but Clem touched my shoulder, and it felt like being splashed with ice water.
"Uhnn, what?"
"Did you find the bones?"
I pointed with my sword. "It's all about the blood pool. I'll bet it's near there. Can we drain it?"
On closer inspection, we discovered that the pool was actually a massive copper bowl filled with, in Clem's estimation, about twenty people. My own blood drained from my head at the prospect, leaving a wave of dizziness. It didn't help that all I could smell was copper and slaughterhouses, my stomach suddenly very glad that I'd skipped breakfast and had been rudely drugged during lunchtime.
"It was nearly twenty-one. Didn't know if you'd hear me. Oh, God, Clem."

I started blubbing, trying to cover my face in my hands. "Aw, I'm sorry, I've been so good."

"You still are." Clem wrapped me in a quick, winged hug. "There's a plug at the bottom, let's get this drained away, all right?"

He tugged on a thin chain, and there was a glug so like that of Nana Sophie's old bathtub that I nearly smiled.

Curiosity had won out over delicacy in Clem. "So, it's an old blood bath system, but with an electrical current running through, and random other occult things added for good measure. Well, it works, but it's rather crude."

"So glad you approve," I quavered slightly.

Clem looked up at me. "You wandered alone and unarmed into a place calling itself the Čachtice Institute. Did that not ring any bells?"

"Honestly, it still doesn't."

"Elizabeth Bathory was one of the first female serial killers. She was said to murder her maids and bathe in their blood to stay young. Nonsense of course, it was simply that contemporary sources couldn't figure out what else a woman would kill for."

"Not being au fait with early serial killers, what's that got to do with Čachtice?" I looked around. "I knew this setup reminded me of a Seventies horror movie."

The blood was down to its last inch or so inside the copper bowl, and Clem started rummaging around in it. "So you aren't aware that Čachtice Castle was her home and later her prison. Well, that makes more se- ah!" He fished a pair of longish bones out of the bottom. "They were glued in. The last two metacarpals, look."

"That's one hell of an anti-slip mat." Something in the next room shattered suddenly, to the sound of female cheering, and I shuddered. "Can we leave now?"

Apocrypha

If you listened carefully, you could hear the battle from here.
Chokkma was alone in the garden now, all other inhabitants expelled for various sins. Sammael's creature had been the last, mutilated and reviled as he crawled in his belly in the dirt. His tongue had been ripped in two so he couldn't bewilder anyone else again, but it made his screams come out as hisses.
Such horror. Chokkma meditated under the Tree, trying to overcome her disgust with understanding. She'd considered eating the fruit, but on closer inspection she discovered the fruit was all rotting. Nothing had ever rotted before, and she didn't care for the smell. Still, it served to remind her that sometimes the long, boring way of acquiring wisdom was better than the quick, exciting way.
And then, she was no longer alone. The angel who stood before her smelled of blood, smoke and sulphur. With an unheard sigh, Chokkma opened her eyes, and gazed at the short figure before her.
"Hello, Iraiel. You look angry."
"But at last, our anger is being heard!" Iraiel drew himself up to his full, if rather modest, height. "Lord Lucifer bids me formally invite you to an alliance against the forces of repression."
"Sam's calling himself Lucifer now? Oh dear." Chokkma stood. "Thank your Lucifer, but tell him that I decline. I'll join with him the moment he sues for peace and ends this terrible conflict."
"But, but you gave Lord Lucifer the idea!" Iraiel had some metal rings linked together to form a long thing like a vine. Chokkma saw the way he gripped it in his fist, and wondered why he seemed so keen on holding heavy pieces of metal."Your

questions, your beliefs! We hold to what you hold to, that's why we fight!"

"If my questions have inspired this horror, then I'm sorry for it. And you have no idea what my beliefs are." Chokkma folded my arms. "Though I imagine you'd cheerfully adapt yourself to my beliefs, if you thought it would get me to go back with you. Don't stand there with your fledgling rage and think I don't see your point. I'm the angel of wisdom, so if I appear in your lines it gives your grievances legitimacy. There'll be desertions, and even the loyal will feel misgivings."

"Yes, yes, that it's exactly! We can win this!" Iraiel raised his chain in triumph.

Chokkma felt a little pity in her heart. "Some of your grievances are real," she said gently, "but there are other ways to express them. You went and listened only to your bloodlust, and now you're killing your own brothers."

"My brothers are only among the free. The rest are merely chattals." Iraiel nearly saluted.

"Are those your words, or Sam's?" Chokkma still spoke softly. "There have been too many mistakes, too much anger, from me as much as anyone, but a better way can be found, will be found. That's my belief."

Chokkma sat back down, and closed her eyes. From his furious splutters, Iraiel was considering something violent, but Chokkma gambled that he'd find that a lot harder to do against someone offering no resistance at all.

A few moments of precious solitude passed, before once more and an angel's scent wafted across to Chokkma. Blood and smoke again, but this time sandalwood was there as well.

"Hello, Ramahael. How's compassion working out for you?"

"Honestly? About as well as wisdom is working out for you." Ramahael scratched his beard, an affectation Chokkma still wasn't used to. "I'm sorry to disturb you."

Chokkma believed him. "I suppose this is an offer of alliance as well?"

Ramahael sat quietly in the grass in front of her. protruding from his belt was a sharp-edged cure of metal, and Chokkma decided she needed to keep up with developments in fratricide.

"It's not so much that we need you, strategically speaking," he explained. "Though every angel to our hand is obviously very welcome indeed. The trouble is, we want to shut this down before the Irin get involved-"

"He wouldn't!" Chokkma shuddered. "No, I take that back. Some excuse is probably being created even now."

"Chok, both sides of this thing are being fought by fanatics. There's no quarter given or asked. We need to bring the war to an end, and if we don't do so soon, then the Irin will end it for us."

She looked Ramahael up and down. "Who, exactly, sent you?"

He grinned through the beard. "Ah, I'm discovered. No, not Gabriel nor Michael nor-what is it?"

"That's it. That's how you stop this." Chokkma kept talking. "Mike was alway the finest warrior of us all, even better than Sam. Have Michael issue a challenge, himself against one champion among the rebels. It'll be Sam, he's too prideful to let someone else soak up the glory."

Ramahael laughed. "A war in which only one more person need die? Very good, wisdom! Remain you then in your garden, while I stop all the Host being massacred."

"Only you could," Chokkma assured him, and closed her eyes.

Long ages passed, while in silence and contemplation Chokkma sat and began to understand. Eventually, once of the things she understood was that she was created as part of a host, and that she needed company.

Cautiously, Chokkma rubbed her eyes open, and stood.

The Tree under which she'd sat for so long was dead, but the Tree of Eternal Life was still clinging to a scraggly windblown form of life. It was the only plant, the rest having been long subsumed by desert.

"It's just your perceptions, Chok," explained a familiar voice.

"Uriel." Chokkma looked him up and down sceptically. "You just happened to be here in this desert?"

He pushed what looked like a long tongue of fire into the sand, and wandered over to her. "No happened about it. I'm the guard here. Well, amongst other things. There are once again four highest in Heaven. Raphael and I were recreated."

"And who are the other two? Did you stand with Gabe and Mike, or did the rebels win?"

"No. And then again, yes." Uriel put a careful arm around her shoulder. "You're thin. Contemplation has made you weak. Will you take bread and fruit?"

"Thank you." Chokkma tasted the small loaf of bread, and decided it was some sort of massive grain. "I've been thinking. Why not give Sam's people a garden of their own? They want to try another way of living, if I understood Iraiel correctly- why did you flinch?"

"I destroyed Iraiel myself. He'd gone mad, biting his own shield, and taking that chain of his to friend and foe alike."

Chokkma gave him a sideways glance. "Is it always your job to give me bad news?"

Uriel kissed her forehead. "Not any more. I will tell you nothing of Lucifer's new and terrible garden, nothing of the world of men, nothing of this desert-"

"This illusion of a desert," smiled Chokkma. "I can see scrubby grassland from the corner of my eye."

"Yes." Uriel matched her smile. "I will say nothing to you except words of rejoicing that you're awake and with me."

Drifting calmly behind Uriel was one perfect cloud. Chokkma saw it, and sighed. Well, it would be safe here, wouldn't it? Safest place in all the world, in fact. "I'm awake, but it's time I got out into the world. It sounds like people need wisdom more than ever. You can ask someone else to guard the garden's gate, if you like."

"Are you asking me to come with you?" Uriel raised an eyebrow.

"Oh, we both know you're going to, I just thought I'd preserve the illusion of choice." She winked at him, and held out her hand. "The mourning's over, my love, and so is the morning. Let's go see what the rest of the day brings, hmm?"

Uriel laughed like a bell rung for the first time, and took her hand.

Chapter Fourteen

The grown ups were arguing.
I knew exactly how Nana Sophie's face would look, it was the fierce expression she'd used when I'd crept home from the pub at night, and according to my father she'd used it when my mother announced her intention to have children.
I'd never seen Clem angry, even when saving me from the copper bath he'd been more amused than fearsome, but he sounded angry now, though his tone was overlaid with something more like desperation.
"My God, Clem, she nearly died!"
These were the first clear words I'd heard. The two of them were downstairs, in the kitchen. I was upstairs, in a spare room that to my knowledge had never been slept in since Nana Sophie moved in. I told myself I wasn't hiding, merely fascinated by the selection of ancient typewriters on her narrow spare bed.
"She's a grown woman, and a human full brimming with free will." Clem had clearly raised his volume to match. "You don't give her, or me, enough credit."
"Clemael," my grandmother's voice was like the last trump. "There is not one creature in the places high and far, the places low and distant, or in the fields we know that can make me afraid. The only thing, the only thing that makes my breath tighten is the thought of what they can do to my little mortal granddaughter."
I burst into tears then, and shame rose hot and red into my face. I'd been so good, hadn't thrown up or fainted, but Nana Sophie being scared because of me, because of what I'd seen, that was too much, like a wall breached in my defences.

"Oh, Helen, love." There was no sound of steps up the stairs, no hand on the bannister, but Nana was there, folding me round in a big hug. "It's all right now. Everything's all right. Who's my little cherub?"

I knew Clem was there before I looked up and saw him. But some rituals are too old to deny. "Me. I'm your little cherub."

"That's right." The affection in Nana Sophie's eyes nearly started me off again. "But what don't you have?"

Again, the answer I'd known since I was a toddler rushed up in a big warm wave of comfort. "I don't have four faces an' eight wings 'an hooves."

"That's right again." Nana Sophie smiled encouragingly.

On a whim, I blinked up at her. "Do you have wings, Nana Sophie?"

Clem laughed like a bright bell at Nana Sophie's confusion. I noticed that there was no sense of them having argued, the storm had clearly passed without leaving a mark.

Nana Sophie gathered her thoughts. "Did Clem tell you?"

"He told me that the only female angel was Chokkma, the Angel of Wisdom. Well, he called you Chok the first day we met, and you hang around with angels, and when I looked up what Sophia meant, it was the Greek word for wisdom." I shrugged, a little sheepish.

"I'll be downstairs," said Clem with frankly unusual tact.

Nana Sophie moved a couple of old Remingtons off the bed so that we could both sit comfortably. Nothing about the way she moved or held herself had changed, but I'd spent a lot of time around Clem and Salve, and realised that if she hadn't been someone I was so very familiar with, I would have pegged her for an angel quite quickly. In my admittedly limited experience, angels move as though being choreographed.

She next to me, and took my hands. "There's so much I've

wanted to tell you, especially since you met Clem. Yes, Helen, I've got wings. Would you like to see them?"

"Yes please," I said, though I've got to admit a few misgivings. It's one thing to guess your Nana is an immortal messenger of someone you're not really sure you believe in, it's another thing to be shown absolute proof.

Nana Sophie rolled her shoulders, and her wings unfolded into view. I stared at them, astonished.

"Wait, you're a barn owl!" I blurted. "I mean, that is, you've got the same brown markings on the outside."

"You'd prefer something more tawny?" Nana Sophie flapped happily, and I saw that the inside of her wings wasn't actually pure white, in fact they had lines of black speckles. "To be fair, screech owls were created first. My wings came later."

Clem seemed slightly puzzled by the proffered wings, and I suppose I couldn't blame him. He was, after all, carrying the standard swan-wing arrangement. "Why did they change to resemble you to owls?"

I could feel my unconscious trying to bring something to my attention. "There was a Welsh lady," I mumbled. "She was all flowers."

"Blodeuwedd," smiled Nana Sophie. "Between her and Lilith, it's a traditional punishment for uppity females." Her smile faded as she took my hands. "Helen, your understanding has come on a lot this past few weeks. I'd like to accelerate that process. Trust me?"

"What are you up to, Chok?" Clem's voice was low.

"I'm going to show her the place of of silk and silver," declared Nana Sophie.

"What?" Clem yelped.

"Oh?" I asked.

Nana Sophie put her wings away, and started moving

typewriters off the bed. "Think of it as a spot of astral travel. And like all astral travel, there's one thing you need to remember. Do not break the silver cord. Whatever else you do, don't break the cord."

I settled down into the space she cleared. "What happens if I break the cord?"

"You'll remain in a persistent vegetative state until your Dad agrees to turn the machine off." Nana Sophie didn't meet my eyes. "It ties your soul to your body, you see."

"Brilliant plan, Chok!" Clem scoffed. "Because of course, she's not faced enough mortal peril for one day."

"And if you'd nearly been sacrificed by insane cultists, wouldn't you want to know why? It's all right for the likes of us, Clem, we can see behind the curtain." Nana Sophie dropped the last typewriter carelessly, and the crash made Clem jump slightly. "Everything's less fearful if only you can understand it."

"You're right there." Closing my eyes, I tried to think of a silver cord. Phantom sensations at my right ankle made me suddenly believe that there was a thin rope or a string knotted in a tight loop just above my foot. I decided not to peek, suspecting that faith in the cord was probably my best idea. "All right, Nana. Show me."

"That's my girl." Nana Sophie put her hand under my head, and lifted me clean out of my own body.

Before the light covered me, my last thought was something reassuring about Clem.

Chapter Fifteen

I stared up at the vaults of Heaven.
For a start, they weren't vaults in the sense that I understood them, in fact from the outside Heaven looked almost like a giant vase, if some giant sea creature could exude frosted glass. There was a definite sense of the organic, but then, compared to all creation, a fancy bit of glassware (albeit glassware on a scale I could only guess as being the size of a city) probably counts as a light pastime. Perhaps Paradise itself was the Grail that the knights of old sought.
"Oh yes," said a cheery voice, "because those waters need muddying further."
I didn't have a body, but whatever was travelling, even if it was just a bobbing light on a silver thread, turned to look at the speaker.
Who looked a bit like, but not entirely identical to, me.
"Hello, Helen," said the girl. "I'm your H.G.A."
"H.G.A?" I'd instinctively backed away.
"Holy Guardian Angel." She smiled winningly, but I've seen a smile very similar to that in the mirror for many years now, and it didn't impress me.
"I didn't realise this place came with a tour guide."
"It doesn't. But you do." She almost swam in the air. I was sure I'd never been that graceful. "I'm your highest self, the part of closest to the divine. The silent self that knows how to uncover the true will of you."
I looked her up and down. "You're pretty chatty for a silent self."
"Well, you have just skipped about twenty years of serious adepting. Amazing what you can do with relatives in high

places."

We both turned to look at the massive vase thing. "Speaking of high places..." I muttered.

"It reminds you of something," said my guide, holy guardian angel, whatever. "What is it?"

"It's the bowl," I heard myself say. "The bowl the ephemerals come out of, and fall back into when they die. This is just a bigger, more complex version, for bigger, more complex angels."

"You're right." My guide was solemn, and it made her voice sound less like me on an answerphone. "Most angels never see it from this angle. Quite a lot of them have never seen the need to leave their cool, clean contemplations for the fractured creation outside the vase, and those that have generally have wings of silk and candlelight. And if you've got wings of silk and candlelight, why would you look at something from below?"

We floated upwards, though floating isn't as purposeful as our approach. The lip of the vase billowed outwards, presumably to provide a circular landing strip for the inhabitants.

"Can we go in?" I was nearly close enough to touch he underside of the lip.

My guide stuck her head over the lid, and grunted her satisfaction. "That's why we're here. The shedu aren't reacting, let's party. Are you going to bob there like the last lightbulb in the shop, or what?"

My frown probably wasn't visible. "Pushy cow, aren't you?" I cleared the rim. "Uh, I should probably watch what I say about cows."

The shedu looked at first glance like bulls. They stood either side of little dips in the lip that led into the interior. The dips reminded me of stone steps that have been used so much that curved dishes have been worn by all the footsteps. The dips weren't the interesting things, though; I was more fascinated by the shedu themselves. Because on second look, the 'bulls' had massive wings, and as they regarded us with bovine placidity, I realised with a little shock that they did so with human heads, beards oiled and curled in a Babylonian style.

"Assyrian, actually," my guide said brightly.

"I bob corrected," I replied dryly. "And stop reading my mind."

"I am your mind!" She made it sound as though being my highest self was some massively worthwhile achievement. "Come on, further up and further in, remember?"

I approached the shedu, who shrugged without interest. "Well," I told the nearest one, "at least we got the C.S. Lewis quote out the way early."

"Could have been worse," rumbled the shedu. "Down the lane they get Dante every single time." Those liquid eyes held a smile at my reaction. "You shouldn't use language like that here, mistress."

"Duly noted," I muttered, and tried not to look so shocked at the talking bull-monster.

My guide was waiting, just kicking at curiously dense cloud formations. "Huh. Just because you can't have walls in heaven, doesn't mean they should fill the place with spiritual candy floss. I bet it's got no calories, either."

"And multivitamins," I agreed. "At least if this is heaven, the dead can eat healthy stuff without it tasting like rice cakes."

"Dead?" My guide looked puzzled for a moment. "Oh, there's no dead people here. This is the wrong bit. If the souls of the virtuous lived in the penthouse suite, we're standing at the back entrance to the kitchens and cellars."

"So good people really come to heaven?" I poked it.

"That's an option, certainly. Tends to be big with monotheists, obviously." My guide wandered into the cloudy confectionery, and her voice muffled a bit. "Everything's an option, when you're human. That's sort of the point of free will. Ah, this looks promising."

Along the ever-spiralling walkways punctuated with fountains and bridges, some angels walked, and some angels flew. But all of them, no matter their power or grace, avoided the statues in the middle.

They were huge, four or five times life size, and utterly forbidding. The two angels were clearly modelled from life, but perhaps using the same model, because they wore identical faces. The one closest to me had his sword raised, adding to his height, whereas the other one was facing the other way, clearly guarding his counterpart's back, and raising one hand as though beckoning- no, ordering reinforcements. The marble used to carve them should have made them look serene, but the expressions, the power of them, made them look severe and judgemental.

"The Irin." My guide spoke quietly. "The twins. They acted as judge and jury of their smaller brethren."

"Who sculpted them?" I took my cue from her, keeping my voice soft.

"Nobody." My guide edged a little closer, and I saw a couple of angel-creatures, like wheels with eye-studded rims, gawk at her slightly. "These are them. In the worst of the battle, the Irin deployed themselves, wiping out entire choirs of angels with a sweep of those swords."

I looked up a the raised weapon again, and found that I could still shudder. "Why did they stop?"

"According to Gabriel, they were in mid swing when they were commanded to hold and wait further instructions. They haven't moved since, they're still waiting."

"Maybe these are their instructions. To stand there and be a monument to the Fall." I wanted to touch them, but I had the idea that the marble would freeze me to the spot. "Every town has war memorials, doesn't it?"

"I hadn't thought of that." My guide bathed me in a big sunlit smile. "Though there's another statue that ended up commemorating the Fall as well."

"Do bits of my spirit really use words like commemorating? Pretty sure I don't even use it for collector's plates."

My guide laughed, and it sounded as though I'd just been included in the best joke in the world. "Then it's probably time you started. Come on, just down this stair case here **staircase**."

I drifted down yet another bannister. "I'm glad I didn't bring my knees along, the disabled access round here is rubbish."

"One pound!" My guide crowed as she rounded a corner.

"What?"

"Every time you use your knees as an excuse to be afraid, I award myself a quid. You might be content to hire a Rover, I'll be buying a Ferrari by the end of the year."

I stopped dead. "Oh, you know what? Screw you. You show up wearing my face and my voice and you act like you're better than me, but you're no use. Now I'm sorry you think I cheated to get into your august presence, but what is you actually want me to do?"

My guide counted points off on her fingers. "Long term, I want you to stop faffing about with other people's dreams, and figure out what yours are. I want you go get off your arse and not opt out because your knees are dodgy. Mostly, I want you to find and connect with your True Will. When was the last time you did something that wasn't someone else's agenda?"

"Oh." I was about to dismiss any talk of a True Will and such as New Age nonsense, but the fact was my grandma's the Angel the Wisdom, and she'd sent my disembodied soul to Heaven so I could have a good mooch round. There comes a point when it's easier to go with the concepts. "And short term?"

"Short term," said my guide, "I want you to come and look at that statue round the corner. I suspect Sophie meant you to see this in particular."

Grumbling, I rounded a corner-and was confronted by an interesting piece of granite. Four interlocking pieces of granite, actually. My guide nodded at them.

"You have to understand, there were four of the angels at first. I mean, the other choirs formed later, but this was the core that all the angels were built around."

This statue was less terrifying then the Irin; for one thing it was pretty much life size. There were originally four figures, but one was draped under a heavy veil and one was smashed off so that only the figure below the knees remained.

"In the early days of humanity, men hunted in groups of four." My guide walked slowly round the statue. "There was of course the Leader, acting as the brain of the group. Then there was the Warrior, who'd probably be the one to make the actual kill. They were the physical side of the equation. On the spiritual side, you'd have the Mystic, who'd appease the animal's spirit, and offer spiritual wisdom to the rest of the party. Finally, the Trickster, who mocked the rest of the group, and the hunt, and in doing so acted like the court jester in later medieval society, telling the unvarnished truth."

I sighed, and wished I had a nose to rub. Well, a nose that I'd been able to bring with me. "So these four original angels were the Leader, Warrior, Mystic and Trickster?" I examined the first two figures more closely, but I was careful not to dislodge the veil off the third. "Hmm. So these are archangels. Uh, so this is

Gabriel, and Michael the Warrior, because Michael took out Lucifer- wait, he must be the Trickster, the one that went seriously off-message." I beamed at my guide. "Someone smashed his image after, right? Which leaves the veiled mystic. Bit weird really, it's not been smashed like Lucifer's, but obviously not someone in favour with the-" I stopped, and bobbed back at a bit. "It's Nana Sophie, isn't it? She'd be the mystic, I mean, being the Angel of Wisdom and all."
"Or, you could have just looked at the plaques." My guide was trying not to grin.
I glanced downwards. "I'm looking, but I'm not reading. Enochian, right? Like the swearwords Nana Sophie used to use when I was little."
"This is where your Nana Sophie came from. This is how she's regarded now."
Looking at the familiar shape, hidden under the fabric I didn't recognise, in a place I could barely comprehend, I felt a wave of homesickness so intense I nearly fell.
"I want to go home!" I nearly wailed it.
"Then that's what we're gonna do." My guide was suddenly decisive. "You don't go back up the way you came in this place. It's ephemerals all the way down."
I pouted. "Not elephants? Elephants are traditional."
There was a distinct sound behind me, that of air moving. It slowed, and I found I could distinguish the individual beats of wings. An awful lot of wings.
"I don't want to look behind me, do I?"
"Oh, I don't know," said my guide carefully, and staring over my blobby glowing form as though her- I mean my- eyes were riveted. "Think of them as a nostalgic piece of your childhood."
I rotated. Standing behind me were two cherubim, and yes, they did have four faces, and eight wings, and hooves. As it goes,

only one of the faces on each cherub was human, but the main impression as that these were not the cute winged babies beloved of chapel frescoes. These were clearly the big scary shock troops of heaven.

"Why are you here?" The cherubim spoke in unison, using their ox-shaped faces for speech.

I thought about raising my hands before I remembered. "Um, I'm sorry. Um, we're leaving now."

"Yes." The first cherub said.

The second one watched me intently. "While you are here, the Metatron must keep silence."

My guide stepped behind me and whispered. "That's the Voice. If a mortal heard it directly, well, there'd be a small glowy puddle on the floor by now."

"And we bear swords, not mops." There was no expression in the first cherub's voice. It says a lot about my social circle that I'd become adept at spotting deadpan angel humour. As it was, both cherubim reminded me a lot of the shedu. Perhaps cherubim evolved from shedu, I thought.

Evolution is for the depths of creation. Say rather that the shedu were a prototype, in this place where nothing good is destroyed.

I gave a big sunny sparkling smile to the cherubim. "Would you excuse me, just a minute? I need to have a word with myself."

"Okay, okay!" My guide threw her hands in the air. "No talking in your head. And as for you two, just point us to the gallery and we'll go."

"You will be watched," intoned the second cherub. The first one didn't speak, just turned and pointed straight-armed at a corridor, his many wings folded around him like a cloak. I really hoped my guide wasn't about to make a crack about the Ghost of Christmas Yet To Come. Instead, she settled for giving him a regal nod and tugging me along.

I could tell when we approached the gallery, the silver thread attached to me suddenly swung in front, leading me off on a glimmering pathway.

"That's okay then," said my guide, touching the thread cautiously. "That means the way we're going is the fastest way to get back to your body."

I gave her a sideways look. "Is that where you're headed?"

"Well, conceptually speaking." My guide waved a hand. "You and I are both separate entities and the same person. Come on, last one to the picture is an archetype!"

The final staircase flattened out, and then the already generous space bloomed out like a blossom from a stalk. The nature metaphor probably arrived in my mind via the carvings around the central pillar. Plants I'd never seen, stone flowers that looked as though they'd intoxicate anyone who sniffed them.

We were clearly at the bottom of the vase. The room was round, not just in terms of the walls but also in terms of the way the walls sloped down to the floor, and the floors in turn sloped up to become that carved pillar. There wasn't a corner in the entire gallery, even the exhibits were in oval frames. Here and there, various angels sat cross-legged in mid-air, meditating on a frame in front of them.

"What are they looking at?" I asked my guide. "The frames are empty."

"Not at all. Stand directly in front of one." My guide bounced over to an unoccupied frame, and beamed at what she saw.

I followed suit, and peered into the frame nearest me. I thought for a moment that it was mirror, there was that same pillar visible for a moment, then the scene blinked and-

And everything was good, all the hurt I'd ever suffered in the past was acknowledged, all in one go, but before the memory

of the hurt could overcome me, it washed away in a wave of warmth and contentment, and nothing could hurt me again and I could stay here forever, warm and safe and utterly treasured by the universe-

My guide was standing between me and the frame. "That's enough Comfort for you, Helen. Come on."

We launched into an undignified scramble all the way down the depths below the gallery. It was still silver-veined marble, still dustless, but nonetheless the level below the gallery was clearly unused. There were piles of objects under silk, and I couldn't help feeling pleased that even Heaven has old junk it doesn't need any more.

"Weapons mostly," said my guide cheerfully. "Gabriel's scythe, Azrael's slightly bigger scythe, Michael's spear, all of that. Or maybe it's a lance."

I felt a little ethereal chill. "Will they need them again in future, then?"

"Eventually, yes. Keep going down here." She wasn't looking at me.

Down I could have worked out for myself, because that's exactly where my silver cord was headed, and I was happy to follow along. Besides, I couldn't shake the idea that the wheel-shaped angels- *the Ophanim*, some stray thought helpfully provided-were still watching us.

Not that my guide had any intention of moving in silence. "You see where the junk wobbles now and then? That's due to the Seraphim, though you can't hear them down here. They're shouting the Trisagion, the Thrice Holy. Sometimes a couple of them start shouting in unison, and everything shakes in sympathy."

I paused. "So between the seraphim and the ephemerals, this whole place is just a giant... praise generator?"

My guide gave me a sharp look. "So? You've been known to turn the music up when you get lonely. Look out in front."

If I had legs, I would have skidded to a halt. Before me was a hole in the floor, a couple of metres across. Edging cautiously towards it, I couldn't see the bottom, except to note without surprise that the silver cord fell right into it.

"This is my exit, huh?" There was a slight breeze picking up, as though trying to push me in.

"Jump," said my guide simply.

I could see how far my cord went down, even bobbing uncertainly on the edge of the pit. "Um, I'm not all that keen."

"Are you all right here? I thought I heard voices." The speaker was shaped like an old man, but old in the sense that everyone hoped for an **and** nobody ever got; healthy and unbowed and a faced so lined it's come back round to being handsome again. He smiled at me with bright eyes, thick white hair and shiny teeth. "I'm Potestas. Can I help?"

One of the Erelim, my guide thought quietly. *They're humble, and all insanely powerful.*

"I'm Helen, it's nice to meet you." Manners never hurt anyone. "I'm trying to get back to my body, I'm a mortal."

He nodded understandingly. "And when you're this far up, your body looks a powerful long way down." He waved a bony hand at my guide. "Any farewells to be made?"

"Oh, right." She stepped in front of me. "Remember, Helen. Your own agenda, and no other."

"My own agenda." I nodded up and down.

"And now..." Potestas took a measured breath.

JUMP.

Chapter Sixteen

With me safely distracted, and Salve off having his wing checked by Poet, Clem told himself that this was as good a time as any to return to the silver temple. It had nothing to do with worrying about my current location. No, not at all.

So far, Clem considered as he ghosted along the winds, we'd been lucky. The greater powers of Heaven and Hell hadn't got involved- well, not to any extent that could be noticed. That was probably Chokkma's influence. She'd always set herself up as a nebulous neutral party. Still, celestial or infernal interference could ruin everything.

Clem looked out over the landscape. *I will heal you all,* he promised silently. *Others may vow to make it better, I will vow to prevent it being bad in the first place.*

He was admittedly faintly surprised when the entrance to the silver temple was where he'd left it. Surely Solomon would have fled by now?

The door opened to Clemael's touch, but he dismissed that as counterweights, and stepped quietly inside.

This time, he was ready for that dazzling interior, stepping easily through the pillars. And this time, waiting on the dais, Solomon braced into a square, heavy throne. It occurred to Clem that if that was solid silver, indeed if even half these objects were more than silver-gilt, then this room represented, quite literally, a king's fortune.

"Clemael." Solomon put out an arm. "You are welcome here. Approach."

Clem took two more steps- then found he couldn't take a third. His legs and wings simply wouldn't obey him, remaining still and heavy.

"Such a simple measure," Solomon nearly purred. "I noticed on your previous visit that you checked ahead, and checked to the side. This time, look up, and then look down."

Clem glanced up at the ceiling, was glad he didn't truly have a stomach. One panel of mirror had been removed from the ceiling, and the whitewashed surface had instead been charcoaled with something similar to the classic seal of Solomon. Clem wondered why it looked different, and tried to read the text around the six pointed star.

"It's backwards..." he whispered, and with a sinking feeling looked downwards.

He was standing the middle of the Seal's reflection.

Clem didn't bother to struggle. Solomon and his assisting jinn had worked their way through the Dukes of Hell, and asked some very searching questions of loyalists as well. Clem suspected that even the four highest might have to surrender to a circle like this.

"Very well," said Clem steadily. "You've caught me. And this is as pleasing a shape as I assume, so you can skip the inevitable request."

Solomon risked a papery smile. "I shall curb my curiosity regarding your other shapes. You're here for the relics."

"My bones, yes." The pressure in the air was changing, it made Clem feel a little uneasy. The smell reminded him inescapably of yellow volcanoes- the yellow being sulphur brimstone. "Oh, no..."

"The trouble is, Clemael," continued Solomon blithely, "that the relics have piqued the interest of another quarter. Note that I wear neither crown nor cap, so that Amaymon may not interfere with his apprentice."

Clem went cold. "But Amaymon's apprentice is-"

A pillar of silver shattered as though made of glass.

"Solomon," bellowed Clem. "No!"

"Solomon," breathed a quiet voice. "Yes."

The dust settled, and a masculine nightmare pranced and reared inside an identical seal to the one holding Clem.. Ram and bull and man were mangled together, haloed with sullen red flames, but instead of hooves or feet the three figures came together in the legs of a giant cockerel.

Solomon sighed, as though reproving a slow student. "Asmodai, human form, if you please."

Clem boggled. "Asmodeus? Here?" Why weren't children screaming in their beds? Why weren't men for miles around shaking with palsy, why didn't the elderly suffer and die in sudden raging madness?

He didn't realise he'd spoken aloud until Solomon answered him. "Because I do not will it to be so. The silver here reflects and contains Asmodai's malevolence."

The demon laughed, a bright, friendly sound, and folded into the shape of a tall, rake-thin monk. "There's no fool like an old fool, is there? Everyone knows you built this place in this manner because your precious Temple wasn't allowed to have anything metal in it. This splendour around us is simple overcompensation."

"You'd surely know about that," muttered Clem.

"Enough." Solomon waved a hand, and a plinth rose from the dais in front of him. Clem's eyes riveted on the slim silver box on the plinth.

"One of you gets the relics," explained Solomon. "And one of you is banished with nothing."

Clem considered rapidly. If he lost here, he could probably do some sort of deal with Asmodai later, though the thought of what he'd have to do for the King of Tartarus made him shudder.

"I propose a trade," Asmodai's voice was still soft. "Give me the relics, and all debts between us will be paid, all grudges settled. Solomon, our vendetta has outlasted the cities I built as your slave. Let us be done, at last."

"Clemael, what have you to say?" Solomon's eyes were glittering with interest.

He's lying, thought Clem. *We're never done with anything, because we don't change. The angels, demons, nephilim, we're all calcified into our habits. I wonder if he' agree to quit his vendetta with Raguel so readily?*

The memory of Raguel's daughter prompted a wild idea. "I have nothing to say, except to wonder if Asmodeus has failed to swyve any good nephilim lately."

The mere thought of Sarah, daughter of Raguel, made Asmodai grin unchastely. "Ah, not recently, but maybe I'll resume my career with your little hawthorn."

Good boy, thought Clem, but allowed panic to fill his features. "Oh no. Solomon, I'll renounce any claim to the bones, in return for Helen being immune to Asmodeus."

Solomon leaned a little way forward, with a distressing creak. "You value one insignificant mortal above all your schemes for the Hand of Mercy?"

"Yes." Clem contrived to sound surprised. "It turns out I do."

"No! No!" Asmodai's monk-shape was starting to blur. "I want the bones! I want the whore! Give me!"

Solomon gestured, and two Jinn, barely more visible then the salamanders they called kin, picked up the slim silver box. "You want what's in here? Really?"

"Yes!" With a tearing sound, Asmodai returned to his nightmare form.

The Jinn drifted steadily across to the still slightly sulphurous circle. Clem held his peace, wondering vaguely what Solomon was up to.

"Give it to me! Now!" Asmodai roared, pounding against the invisible pressure of the seal.

The two jinn flipped open the box- and even from his angle, Clem could see there were no bones in there. Instead, it looked like two small pieces of offal. Asmodai screamed, more in rage than pain, and, still twisting around in mid-air, vanished from view.

"Fish heart and fish liver," pronounced Solomon in satisfaction. "The smoke from their heating will banish and repel him all the way to Egypt. Jinn are made of fire, and silver is an excellent thermal conductor."

Clem sagged. "Can I go now?"

"Oh yes- along with your relics. You chose wisely, Clem, and you make a better guardian for them than Asmodai ever would."

"Thank you," murmured Clem humbly, careful to keep his eyes downcast in case Solomon saw the triumph in them. It wouldn't do to ruin a perfectly good lie at this late stage.

The jinn streaked upwards, leaving pairs of scorch marks all over the seal, breaking its integrity. Clem stepped forward, delighting in his ability to do so, and wasn't surprised when a third jinn produced a small scroll case that rattled promisingly.

"You'll forgive me," said Clem dryly, "If I ask that the case be opened ten feet from me."

Solomon smiled, like a fold in a tax demand. "Of course." Surprisingly, he opened the scroll case himself, with a little cardboard popping sound. "No fingers, all the matter near the wrists instead."

Clem nodded. "Why did you open it, and not the jinn?"

"Because they're innocents." Solomon raised his chin. "The sinless animals of the angelic world."

Clem tried not to splutter. "Er, jinn? Sinless? Seriously?"

"Well, perhaps not the jinn." Solomon's lip thinned in what was either amusement or disapproval. "But the elementals themselves indicate an angelic ecosystem." The chariot rolled silently towards Clem. "Perhaps I should refresh my studies into your nature."

Clem tried to back away as far as the circle permitted. "Well, you've had my bones these last few centuries, that's the only opportunity you're getting."

"Perhaps so." Shockingly, Solomon produced a bulky matte pistol. "But I've no doubt I'll judge you yet, Clemael." He raised the pistol- and with a popping little 'ptoo' sound, the pistol shot out a paint pellet that splashed against the circle painted on the ceiling.

Clem stretched his wings, rather gracelessly snatching the scroll case. "Thank you."

"You're welcome, I'm sure." Solomon started rolling backwards, back up the dais. "The exit is to your left."

Chapter Seventeen

I woke, drooling lightly into a pillow.
Clem smiled into my fluttering eyes. "I reckoned you got back all right when the snoring started."
I smiled sleepily up at him, making a mental note to wake up next to Clem more often. "I'm a smug bitch, aren't I?"
"From time to time." Clem's kiss swept lightly onto my cheek. "I'm glad you're all right. Cho- Sophie's on her third cup of tea, I'll see if I can get you one."
I watched his retreating back, looking as human as I'd ever seen it. And I wondered, over and over again, about agendas.

"...so Salve has the jar, he's taken it back to your house." Clem was scrolling through the texts on my mobile. "I might go and see if any of his people have a shortcut to fixing his wing."
I sipped my glass of milk at Nana Sophie's kitchen table, wishing I'd waited for the kettle to boil. "I got bones, Salve got bones, you got bones. Is that all of it now?"
"Oh yes." Clem's eyes glittered. "Everything will change once...oh, Helen, I've waited so long."
He sounded like a child on Christmas Eve, but his face was more like a fanatic admiring the belt-bomb. I covered my sudden unease with another sip.
"So, I guess we're assembling them tonight?"
"I think so. Truthfully, I'm only off to Cornwall to delay my pleasure. I'll see you soon." With a soundless beat of wings, Clem vanished from sight.
I sat there, deflated. On the one hand, it was a pleasant change for Clem to actually reveal his emotions, on the other hand...if I was being as honest as I'd so stridently advised myself to be,

then frankly I was a bit disappointed that Clem's pleasure wasn't, well, me.

I was mercifully distracted by a sudden small sunrise, and Nana Sophie appeared in all her winged and youthful splendour.

"What do you think?"

"Did you put angel of vanity of your CV?" I stuck my tongue out at her.

"Cheeky sphinx." Nana Sophie laughed, and sat down.

"So," I said eventually, when the silence started getting to me. "Why'd you leave the other angels?"

Every time I looked at Sophia, she got a little younger. Nothing dramatic, just a wrinkle growing shallow, a hair turning blonde from grey. In the light she cast, her hair must have looked the same colour as her wings. "Do you know what ephemerals are?"

"Salve told me once, actually. Long car journeys, you know how it is." I took a sip of milk. "There's a cauldron. It's full of raw firmament- the primal stuff that creation's made out of. And all the time, the cauldron bubbles. The bubbles rise, become these tiny, sentient angels called ephemerals. They're beautiful, no harm to anyone, they just bob up and down and sing hymns of praise all day long in joyful voices. Then, at the end of their day, they pop like bubbles, and tumble back into the cauldron, all the while jostled by their brothers and sisters who, also, will only live one day." I didn't ask the question that was forming, not when I saw her face.

Nana Sophie stared down at her mug of tea. "That's about the size of it. And I always thought, 'what's the point of that, then? Why have angels born to die after just one day?' I realised it in the end, it's all about having a renewable source of people telling you how great you are. it's just a giant egowank."

I giggled despite myself. You don't expect your nice middle-class granny to swear like that.

"Well, it is." Sophia smoothed out her skirt. "That got me thinking, and looking round at the other angels, and at myself, and I realised, that bar a bit of fetching and carrying that's what all the angels were. So I publicly denounced- oh, a lot of things, I was having a proper adolescent strop by this point- and left the place of angels under my own steam."

By now, Sophia looked the same age as me. Why do angels default to mid-twenties? "So, you didn't get involved in the fall?" I asked "You said something about the old firm and its squabbles."

"Exactly." She lifted up her hair, now entirely ash-blonde. "I came here, spent a long time meditating. I wonder sometimes, if maybe my little strop inspired a larger Fall, but no, that's just hubris." She smiled wanly. "I'm told both sets of angels came to seek my help, and found me in the first garden, unresponsive under a tree. First thing I knew about it was when I woke up, saw Uriel and asked how long I'd been thinking." She sighed. "All a bit of a cockup, really."

I fiddled with the edge of the tablecloth. "Solomon is your son, then. Which I guess makes him my uncle."

"I bedded David, King of Israel. Or he bedded me, either way. Marriage vows were not his strong point, that boy." I could see Nana Sophie fighting a misty haze of recollection. "And being fair, he was certainly under no obligation to acknowledge his misshapen bastard, much less have him king after him. I wish you two could have met under better circumstances." Nana Sophie walked away. "I can only guess he's disgusted at you consorting with a fallen angel?"

"Oh, come on," I protested. "Salve isn't so bad. And not technically fallen."

"Salve isn't technically fallen," agreed Nana Sophie, "but Clem

certainly is."
Everything stopped for me, just for a moment.
"Clemael? You're saying the Angel of Mercy is fallen? Condemned to hell as a demon?" There were more things I had to say, but I couldn't get them out, not through the way my throat tightened. The best I could manage, to my shame, was a wail of "He tricked me, Nana! He did!"
Nana Sophie looked at me compassionately. "My word, you're very upset about this. Are you bedding Clem?"
I sniffled a denial.
"But you'd like to? You're not too keen on sex, as I remember."
I looked up at her, aghast. There's some things you just don't discuss with your Nana. But that, I decided, was just a way of looking at things. Discussing them with the angel of wisdom, on the other hand, wasn't so bad. After all, she hadn't so much been around the block as written helpful little notes in the margins of the blueprints used to build the block.
"It's not that I'm not keen on the principle, thank you very much. It's just, frankly it's disgusting. Both parties sweat, and ooze things, and if you're not careful the ooze makes you either pregnant or diseased or both. Even if you are careful it might do that, actually. Ugh. It's just really unsanitary. There's things...suppurating. Gives me the cold shudders."
"Well, thank you for that mental image." Nana Sophie smiled. "You've probably just made the nephilim extinct."
I squinted at her. "You've just turned the subject away from me having a right royal tantrum, haven't you?"
"You were starting to shred the tablecloth, yes." Nana Sophie sighed. "Talk to Clem. He's the same person you hope to not suppurate with. Talk to him, Helen."
"Hmph, I replied.

Chapter Eighteen

"Salve, mate," I called, throwing my keys onto the sofa. "Need you out the house for an hour or so."
Salve wandered into the living room. I was sure where he'd got the pale green shirt, but it suited him. "I can do that! Ooh, you're an oncoming storm tonight. Why such thunder?"
"You're best out of it, I'm not angry at you." I opened my purse, and then a small bag from the art shop. It held a craft knife, and a stick of chalk. "Here's a twenty, get yourself to the pictures."
Salve took the proffered money. "I'll be home for midnight. Be careful, whatever it is that you're up to."
"Much too late for that," I told him grimly.

Twenty minutes later I was finished, and there was a knock at the door. Funny, how well I'd come to recognise his knock. Sick to my stomach, I dragged myself over to the door, and answered it, stopping to check a discreet piece of electrical tape on the way.
It was, of course, Clem at the door, and as soon as the door opened I knew I couldn't look him in the eye.
"You've come for the jar, then."
"That's right," he said cheerfully, strolling into my hallway as though he wasn't a lying demon bastard. "We have all the pieces now, time to assemble the Hand of Mercy."
At that moment, something died just under my ribs. The Hand of Mercy. He wasn't even pretending to simply be re-attaching the limb. For a second, half a second, I felt an insane urge to tell him what I'd done, but that died too. I looked at that that fluffy hair and those dove-grey gloves and understood I couldn't even hate him properly.

Clem caught something of my mood. "Helen? Are you all right?"

"You made me think you were a good angel. But really you're a demon. You lied to me. You're not really the Angel of Mercy." Too many emotions jostled onto Clem's face. "I am still the Angel of Mercy. It's just that I'm...freelance, these days."

"Oh, what?" The anger flared in me, hot and fast, before falling back.

"We had our reasons, many different ones, when a third of us rebelled." Clem unconsciously hugged himself. "In my case, I'd vowed to liberate a slave race. Chokkma was right; the ephemerals, and the angels in general, we were vanity's ornaments. So I rose up with my fellows, and laid waste to my brothers in an attempt to free them."

"By killing them for freedom?"

Clem was sombre. "I didn't think it would come to that. Helen, we were outnumbered two to one, and the other side had what you might call the big guns. I honestly didn't think we'd get near enough to do them any harm. And I already knew we couldn't win. But I could die a free angel, one of the few there had ever been, I could be a martyr, and perhaps an inspiration to the other angels."

Clem sat heavily on the sofa. "In other words, I replaced another's vanity with my own, I suppose. But when the battle was over, and the fallen condemned, I grew to believe that while too many of us sank to apathy, or tupenny temptations, I could still do the work I loved, I could still dispense mercy, just under my own auspices."

I still couldn't look at him. "No wonder you're scared of the underground. Too much like your punishment, was it? Why don't you have bat wings, anyway?" I could hear the whine in my voice. "Why do you still look like you're good?"

Where a human might have looked wounded, Clem's face became smooth and expressionless, placid as a plaster statue. "If you raised a spear to your brothers, would your hair uncurl, or your freckles vanish?" He stood. "Can I have my hand back now?"

I reached under the sofa, and produced the jar. "Sure. I mean, I could withhold it, but you'd smite me, or trick me, or do something dreadful to me to get this jar back. And I'd just as well skip the unpleasantness."

He took the jar, still ostensibly serene as a Jersey cow. "And that is how you now see me. Despite all that's happened. Despite all we've...seen." He brightened slightly. "Well, when the Hand of Mercy is complete, I'll give it to a human magician- if there's one thing you've taught me, it's how very imaginative humans can be- on the understanding that he or she will undo this sad misunderstanding. That's what it does, you see. The Hand of Mercy, it allows you to liberate a person from the consequences of their mistakes. That's the greatest mercy, you know, being able to undo great evil before it happens." As he spoke, Clem unpeeled the crystal hand from his wrist with a slight sound that reminded me of a suction cup. Shaking the bones out of the jar, he picked a few tiny pieces out, and started adding the bones onto his wrist. I wasn't surprised to see the flesh grow, translucent as moonlight, over the replaced bones.

I needed to distract him, but the appalled tone in my voice was entirely genuine. "You're going to give someone the power of Control-Z over the whole universe? Clem, humans perceive in linear time, if you destroy the laws of cause and effect we'll go crazy and die. You're wiping out the human race with that thing."

"Not at all!" He beamed, adding on another finger. "Humanity will be saved from all evil, that's true mercy." The bones were jumping out of the jar on their own now, as though some sort of critical mass was being reached.

"Don't you see?" I nearly pleaded. "Solomon knew it too, that's why he tried to stop you."

"Solomon has simply lost his sanity in the face of all my fallen brothers he's hunted and trapped over the ages." The fingernails started to form over the restored flesh. "You're witnessing a wonderful thing, Helen."

"No," I said simply. "I'm really not."

I wanted to close my eyes, but I didn't want to miss this for anything in the world. After all, what was about to happen was probably unique in the annals of history.

Clem held up the completed hand. It was exactly how I pictured it, thin and pale and probably very musical. "Well then, let's try it on something small. Your unhappiness at my fallen state should do."

He moved the hand in a complicated gesture, as though giving an elaborate benediction. There was a flash- then a smell of burning schools.

"It's wrong!" Clem shrieked. "What's happened?"

I looked at him, and knew that my face and voice would give nothing away. "You deceived me, Clemael. I didn't like that. I thought human bone would be too dense, and that you'd spot it, so I took a piece of chalk and carved it in the shape of your trapezium bone. One of the little ones, to make it less noticeable. There is no Hand of Mercy."

Clem stared at me. "Where's the original bone?"

"You see this broken white dust on the carpet?"

Clem wailed, a hopeless defeated sound. Then he brought his hand round, the hand he and I had spent so many weeks assembling, and he smashed the back of it into my face so forcefully I fell back, over the sofa, and where my head hit the wall there was no sound at all.

Chapter Nineteen

I wasn't aware of being unconscious. But Clem was gone, and Salve was asking me to look at his eyes.
"You weren't supposed to be back yet." My voice sounded quiet and far away.
"It's half past midnight at least," Salve told me. "And let me tell you, the queen of concussion reigns at the side of your skull. Hmm. Let's see." He carefully didn't move my head, which probably should have worried me. "There's another bruise forming on the opposite side of your head, which is fingermark-shaped."
"It's chalk." I assured him earnestly.
His brows knotted "The chalk fought back? Deep dark, Helen, don't even confront the watercolours!"
"No," I snapped, skittish and angry at the sudden wash of head pain. "I'd never hurt his bones, the dust is where I carved the chalk, is all."
"You need medical attention, right now." Salve stood. "I've done what I can, but honestly? I'm really worried. I used your travelling telephone to call for an ambulance."
"Don't tell him it's taped under the table! He mustn't know!" I grabbed Salve's shirt, frantic. He sighed, and touched the centre of my forehead gently. A great wave of painless calm spread over me, and I sank back into it gratefully.

Everyone should have a walking painkiller like Salve. The actual healing I had to do by myself, but Salve's touch kept me lucid enough for the triage nurse at A&E to correctly diagnose concussion, and after a few hours sent me home. She looked at the bruise where Clem hit me, and I advised her tersely that I just dumped someone that night. I could hear her muttering under her breath that it clearly wasn't a moment too soon.

Salve met me with a taxi, and seeing him the unforgiving lights of A&E's reception made me realise just how well he'd adapted above ground. He wouldn't win any glamour awards, granted, but nobody gave the apparent teenager with the lank hair and the wide eyes any real notice.

"Clemael called for you while you were out," Salve sounded tired. "I told him where you were- but don't be scared, I didn't say which bit of the hospital, and I only did it to make him feel bad."

I felt nausea build, and I hoped it was simply concussion. "Is he gone now?"

"Yes, he ran like he was robbing a bank.." The words were gloating, but the tone was not. "You need rest and care, not worrying about him."

"I do worry, and I do c-"

The taxi swerved, and Salve instinctively put out an arm to protect me from being buffeted. Luckily, we were both wearing our seatbelts.

I could hear the taxi driver swear in a language I didn't know, then "Get your buggy out the way, old man!"

I put my hands over my eyes. "Anyone else want to guess who that is?"

Salve stuck his head out the window. "Ah, yeah. I thought he'd left us all dangling on the rope too long." He coughed, and stepped out of the halted taxi. "Hail to you, King Solomon."

Salve head left the taxi door open. I perched half in, half out, and tried to decide if my head hurt more than my knees. I let the concussion do the talking, and flashed a watery smile at the driver. "Sorry about this. Family's always embarrassing, you know?"

"Little cousin," called Solomon. "I did warn you about the Hand of Mercy. It was awoken briefly at your home tonight. I believed myself too late to stop it."

"You were," I snapped. "And I've got the hospital notes to prove it. And I'm your bloody niece, not your cousin."

Solomon smiled, a thin line on parched lips. "And you sound more like my mother each day. Come, sister's daughter, we go to confront the perpetrator." He saw my look. "Don't be feared. He will not hurt you again."

"I don't want to hurt him again," I replied softly.

Solomon rolled his chariot a little further. "What must be, must be. I am Judgement to his Mercy."

"No, mate," I sighed, walking towards the chariot. "You're a descendant of Wisdom, same as me. Let's see if that works better. Coming, Salve?"

Salve muttered something in Enochian. I pretended not to know what it was.

Chapter Twenty

Three of us on the chariot was an awkward affair. This close to Solomon, I figured out that all that was holding him together was some impressive, though discreet, corsetry. It basically acted as a primitive scaffold. His leg braces were bolted into hidden parts of the chariot, tying man and machine together with thick rusted rivets.

Salve and I opted to cling to Solomon, and each other and the chariot all at the same time, so it was a slightly undignified bundle of nephilim and fallen flesh that rolled up in front of All Saints, the town's biggest church,. My Dad used to take me here for Christmas when I was younger, it seemed odd not to be here in midwinter.

"Holy ground?" I looked up. "Can he even do that? I remember...he flinched at the chapel in Isham house. Can he just stroll in when it's still consecrated?"

"Not lightly," advised Solomon. "Not without pain. The beauty and the numinous of even the most humble chapel must remind him of what he's lost."

"Perhaps he's being all, you know, penitent?" Salve suggested. "I think I'll remain out here."

Solomon shot him a haughty look. "I'm not surprised, Healer."

"Manners," I said to nobody in particular.

As we pulled up to All Saints, I was surprised to see the door unlocked and open. Considering how late it was at night, that struck me as either an open invitation for the homeless to doss down, or else angelic intervention.

I huddled deeper into the chariot. There's a time and a place for being brave, but I wasn't much inclined towards bravery when about to step into a darkened building to face a demon who'd recently slammed me into a wall.

"Will you be afraid forever?" Solomon started guiding his chariot forward.

"...maybe," I admitted.

My uncle handed me a worn leather rein that appeared attached to the foremost rivet of the chariot. "Correct. Unless you temper your fear tonight."

And so we went into the dark.

When I think of a church, my mind mentally furnishes it with big old candles, and maybe strips of electric light competing feebly. There was nothing like this, no illumination except for a thin gold glow behind the altar.

Solomon and I exchanged wordless glances. Once I got my eye in I saw that the glow was more of a sickly yellow, getting on for mustard, and my ears chose that moment to mention the muffled sobbing.

"Clemael," called Solomon, making the most of the church's acoustics. "Come forth. Hear my judgement."

There was no response.

"Clem," I called softly, and was rewarded by a slightly louder sob that make my chest squeeze slightly.

As far as either Solomon and I could tell, Clem hadn't actually moved. I tapped my uncle's hand, and twirled a finger round. He nodded briskly, and I slipped out of the chariot, and circled my way round the altar as quietly as possible.

Clem wasn't actually dishevelled as such. I guess someone created to be as beautiful as an angel couldn't get properly ragged. But in his old hand he carried the small hammer I kept for putting up shelves, and his new hand was a mass of circular bruises.

"I can't bring myself to hit hard enough." He said.

I mentally dialled back the conversation to levels I used for Mr.

Asherwood. "Did you hurt yourself?"
He looked up at me. The tears of angels, as it transpired, weren't made of light after all, It's just commonplace salt water, just like the rest of us.

"I did you harm, with this hand." The vulnerability dropped out of his voice, leaving something colder and fiercer. "So this hand, the Hand of Mercy, must be destroyed. The bones must be crushed to powder, like you showed me." He raised the hammer again. "I am an angel. I have no business harming humans. This is my rightful punishment." I don't think he noticed when I gently snatched the hammer out of his still-raised hand.

"Stop now," I told him. "Judgement isn't your job. It's Solomon's."

"Clemael," thundered Solomon, "Now hear my judgement. You have wronged this woman, in several different ways. Therefore, I place your life at her disposal."

He didn't even protest, slumped on the floor like a forgotten toy. "Truly, you are the wisest of judges."

"Reach down, and look up." I bobbed a little, and wasn't at all surprised to find a sword pommel brush against my fingers. It was the brittle facsimile I'd used in the Institute, but it was sharp enough to take off someone's head. I don't know if Clem heard the thought, but he knelt, and lifted his chin.

"Helen?" It was just a whisper, and with all my attention on the sword in my hand I wasn't sure who'd spoken. Clem watched me take a firm grip on the blade and brace myself.

There was complete silence. But not a church silence, when the last note of the hymn dies away, and the organist rests. This was the jagged silence that happens when people realise they can't stop a terrible thing from happening.

And the first time, I finally understood what my True Will was.

I raised the sword- and slammed the point into the flagstone before Clem. He jumped, nearly falling sideways, as sparks flew from the impact of metal on stone. The blade went in a good six inches, which shouldn't have been possible with human strength.

"This is what it takes to be the hand of mercy." I didn't recognise my own voice. "The hand of mercy does not simply drop the blade and do nothing. The hand of mercy does not swing for a painless kill. The hand of mercy takes the killing blade, and finds a better use for it. This time tomorrow, Birch and Poet will be forging this into a ploughshare."

I sighed, and felt some of the certainty fall out of me. "I don't even know what a ploughshare looks like, mind, but I'm going to find out, and I'm going to hang it on my wall."

There was a dusty smacking sound, and then another. Solomon applauding. "You did say we'd try wisdom instead of judgement. But judgement has been made, and his life is yours."

"I know." My headache was coming back, and I was exhausted. "But you seriously can't take the life I just spared."

With an ominous creak, Solomon drew himself to his full height. "You cannot gainsay my judgement. You presume too much, woman."

I managed to suppress the incipient temper tantrum, but it cost me a deep breath. "I'm sorry, but I'm not presuming. You're as bound by the rules as angels are, aren't you? That's got to be the price of your immortality. Well, under the rules, Clem's been spared. You can't execute him. Look, if his life's mine, why not release him to my custody? I'll keep an eye on him, make sure he doesn't bugger about with cause and effect any more."

Solomon coughed once, a sound as dry as tearing vellum. "Clemael, hear now the wisdom of Solomon. Too long have you divided your your loyalties, like a motherless baby, between Heaven and Hell. So for the next one hundred years from this very hour, your loyalty is to be to Helen Hawthorn. You will enter her service for the rest of her life, and then stand vigil over her grave for the remainder of the hundred years."

"I don't want a slave!" I yelped in protest. But at the same time, a colder part of me was thinking: nice move, Solomon. If you'd enslaved him for the rest of my life, he'd hit me a lot harder next time.

In the time I thought that, Clemael got on his knees in front of me. "Let me serve."

I looked up at the partly hidden ceiling, and even in the dimness caught some sense of intricate beams, and ornate plasterwork. There were some tiny cherubs blowing vague-looking trumpets in the corners, and they reminded me of what someone had once said. Angels are made to preserve. And obey. And sing in adoration.

"Oh, fine," I grumbled, "if it keeps you out of trouble. But no more kneeling, my joints are trying to cramp in sympathy. And you're not calling me mistress, either, I haven't got the corsets for it."

That ripping vellum sound again, and I understood that Solomon was trying not to laugh. A tiny, tiny smile tried its path across Clem's face as well.

"Don't worry, Helen, corsets could be arranged."

Chapter Twenty-One

So from being vast and empty, my flat became small and cramped. Salve already lives in the spare bedroom, when he's not attending college. He brings home brochures about nursing qualifications, and tries to figure out if he can afford it. Since he lives rent free and has a liking for food, rather than a necessity for it, his expenses shouldn't be too horrendous. Clem, meanwhile, sleeps on the sofabed, but none of us are pretending that's going to last much longer. Last night he and I watched a late film, and I woke up seven hours later still on the sofa, one arm still loosely wrapped round his waist. He wisely didn't mention it- it's taken a while to rebuild trust between us, and I still haven't told him about the hidden bone. Last time we refitted a plug socket I dropped it into the cavity wall insulation. Maybe archaeologists will find it in a couple of hundred years' time.

I don't know what I'm going to do about the shop. Sitting quietly among the same antiques day after day, I'm starting to feel like a particularly rococo Pharaoh. It's hard to keep it going, when I'm still young and there's a world full of interesting things I could be doing. But still, it can't all be quests and demons and mad cultists.

Leave perfection to the angels. This'll do me.

Epilogue

There is, of course, just one last thing.

I know little Helen spends enough time around Asherwood to assume age equals senility, but surely when she sees her dear old grandmother being harmless and helpful, an alarm should sound?

I keep expecting her to ask the question. "Nana Sophie, if Sir Elgar lived four hundred years ago, how come his poem referenced a big gold spear that was made five years ago? And how come everything was where he said it was, and hadn't been moved in centuries?"

I was rather proud of that, actually, though I'm not sure about that last couplet. Still, I had about five minutes to scribble it down before Clem arrived for tea. Helen arrived right on cue, bless her- I can only assume she gets that punctuality from her Dad, point me to a decent garden and me that's distracted for about a year- and everything went more or less to plan.

So now humanity is safe, Solomon owes me for slipping him the last lot of bones, Clem's wings are clipped, and Helen is shaping up nicely. I wonder how much time she has remaining?

I suppose there's one important lesson I took from meditating in Eden. When you're the Angel of Wisdom, there is no retirement.

Thank God.

About The Author

Ni Claydon was born in 1979 in Oxfordshire. In 2001 she failed to become a cosmic space-baby, but did gain a BSc in Information Systems (Artificial Intelligence). She now lives in the East Midlands and has a desperately unremarkable day job. Hand of Mercy is her first novel, though she has written a one-shot comic for Accent UK.